DAWN SAVES THE PLANET

**Other books by
Ann M. Martin**

*Rachel Parker, Kindergarten Show-off
Eleven Kids, One Summer
Ma and Pa Dracula
Yours Turly, Shirley
Ten Kids, No Pets
Slam Book
Just a Summer Romance
Missing Since Monday
With You and Without You
Me and Katie (the Pest)
Stage Fright
Inside Out
Bummer Summer*

BABY-SITTERS LITTLE SISTER series
THE BABY-SITTERS CLUB mysteries
THE BABY-SITTERS CLUB series

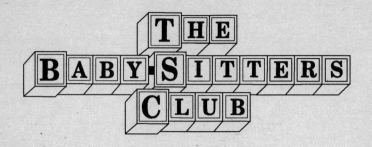

DAWN SAVES THE PLANET

Ann M. Martin

AN
APPLE
PAPERBACK

SCHOLASTIC INC.
New York Toronto London Auckland Sydney

*The author gratefully acknowledges
Jahnna Beecham and Malcolm Hillgartner
for their help in
preparing this manuscript.*

Cover art by Hodges Soileau

ISBN 0-590-92583-0

12 11 10 9 8 7 6 5 4 3 2 1   11   6 7 8 9/9 0 1/0

Printed in the U.S.A.   40

CHAPTER 1

"Do you think kids can save the planet?"

That was the question my science teacher Mrs. Gonzalez asked my class at Stoneybrook Middle School today. Most of the class just sat there like lumps staring at her.

But not me. I raised my hand and practically shouted, "Yes, of course!"

I'm Dawn Schafer. I'm thirteen years old and have been known to be pretty outspoken when it comes to environmental issues or organic food. My friends in the BSC (Baby-sitters Club) say I'm a health food nut, just because I don't eat junk food and red meat. (The sight of a hot dog makes me want to gag!) But my mom and I have always eaten healthy things like raw vegetables, tofu, and brown rice. We feel better because of our diet.

Mary Anne, my stepsister, is the complete opposite of me. She's not a junk-food addict, but she does like cookies and candy and hamburgers and French fries, and so does her dad, Richard. Which makes meals at our house pretty crazy.

Guess what. I'm not from around here. I was born in California. So how did I get to Stoneybrook, Connecticut? Well, you see my mom was born here but years ago she moved to California, where she met and married my dad. Unfortunately, things didn't work out between them. When they got divorced, she brought me and my brother Jeff back to Stoneybrook.

At first, I didn't like Stoneybrook very much, but things really changed after I met Mary Anne. We became instant best friends, even though we're as different as night and day. She's short, with brown eyes and brown hair. I'm tall with white-blonde hair that comes down to my waist, plus I've got blue eyes.

Mary Anne is sort of preppie when it comes to clothes. She wears pleated wool skirts and neat white blouses, stuff like that, while I have my own style of dress that my friends in the BSC call California Casual.

Speaking of the BSC, right after I met Mary Anne, she introduced me to her friends in the Baby-sitters Club. They asked me to join and now the BSC is one of the most important things in my life.

Now here's the really weird part: Mary

Anne and I discovered that our parents had been in love when they were in high school (we found it out by reading their yearbooks). But they ended up marrying other people. Mary Anne's mom died when she was really little and her dad, Richard, had to raise her all by himself. He was pretty strict for most of those years, but now all that has changed.

Anyway, once Mary Anne and I discovered that our parents had been high school sweethearts, we decided to get them back together. And we did! Isn't that cool?

Then our parents got married (after dating *forever*) and now Mary Anne is not only my best friend, but my stepsister, too. Unfortunately, my brother Jeff got homesick and moved back to be with my father in California. I miss him a lot, but he's much happier with his friends and the warmer weather. It can get super cold here! Especially in the drafty old farmhouse we live in. It's over two hundred years old and even has a secret passage leading from the barn to my room. I'm not sure, but I think it could be haunted.

Things were really crazy at our house after our parents got together. Mary Anne and I discovered that even though we liked each other a lot, we have very different habits. For instance, I *have* to listen to music when I study. Mary Anne needs complete silence. And like

I said before, I'm totally into health food. Mary Anne could take it or leave it. Plus, I'm outgoing and a little impulsive. Mary Anne is on the shy side.

Then there're our parents, who are also complete and total opposites. My mom is the ultimate slob. Washing dishes or cleaning the house are about the last things she wants to do, whereas Mary Anne's dad is Mr. Organized-Neat Freak. Everything in his life is labeled, including the socks in his dresser. (I may be exaggerating just a little bit.)

Even though Mary Anne and I are really different in many ways, there are a lot of things we agree on. Like helping the environment. I know if Mary Anne had been in Mrs. Gonzalez's class, she would have raised her hand and said, "I agree with Dawn. We *can* save the planet if we all pull together."

Anyway, after I made my announcement in class, Mrs. Gonzalez folded her hands in front of her and smiled at me. "Dawn is right. You can help save this planet, even if you are young. And a good place to start is in your home, or school, or town."

Mrs. Gonzalez, who is very cool and has long dark hair that she wears in a thick braid down the center of her back, pointed to the posters she had thumbtacked over the blackboard.

"I've listed things that are going wrong with the environment at this very moment. Dawn, would you read them out loud?"

All of the kids in the room turned to look at me, and Alan Gray, possibly the most disgusting, immature boy in the eighth grade, crossed his eyes. I tried to ignore him and read the headings to the rest of the class. "Acid Rain and Air Pollution."

"Invisible gases are released by cars that burn gasoline, and power plants that burn coal," Mrs. Gonzalez explained. "These gases can mix with water and make it highly acidic. When these gases get into rain and snow clouds, the acid falls back to the earth, destroying trees and polluting the water in our lakes and rivers. Air pollution also makes it difficult for us to breathe."

"Vanishing Animal Life," I continued reading.

"As more and more people are born," Mrs. Gonzalez said, moving down the center aisle of the class, "more and more forests are cut down to make room for them. The areas where wild animals can live are replaced by homes and stores, and the animals become extinct."

I wrinkled my nose as I read the next heading. "Too Much Garbage."

"When people throw things away, the garbage gets buried in the ground or thrown in the ocean." Mrs. Gonzalez stopped by my desk and crossed her arms. "Pretty soon there won't be any more room for our garbage. So what can we do about it?"

Once again I raised my hand. "Recycle."

"That's right." Mrs. Gonzalez patted me on the shoulder and this time Alan stuck his tongue out at me. Sometimes I can't believe how immature he acts.

"Recycling means reusing paper and glass and aluminum over and over again." Mrs. Gonzalez returned to the front of the class and tapped the last poster. "And the final heading is what?"

"Water Pollution," I read.

Mrs. Gonzalez nodded. "Every living creature depends on water to survive. But our oceans and rivers are polluted by garbage, and much of the water we drink is being wasted. We need to keep it clean."

Then she pointed to another poster. This one was completely blank.

"Class, your assignment for this grade period is to pick one of these topics and design a project that can help to save our planet. We'll list them on this poster."

Everyone began to talk at once, announcing which category they were going to choose. A couple of groans came from the back of the class but most of the students sounded pretty excited about our new project.

The noise was so loud that Mrs. Gonzalez had to shout to make her last announcement heard. "You have one week to come up with an idea for your project and hand in a brief description of what you plan to do." The bell rang and she called, "See you tomorrow!"

I gathered my books, keeping an eye on the posters at the front of the room. My brain was already clicking away. I spent the next hour thinking about ecology. (It's a good thing I was not called on in social studies, because my mind was not on the French Revolution.) With so many possibilities to choose from, I realized it was going to be hard to pick just one project.

I decided to discuss the assignment with my friends at lunch. Claudia Kishi and Kristy Thomas were already seated at our regular table when I reached the cafeteria.

It's not hard to spot Claud. She dresses in ultra bright colors that look great with her jet black hair. She likes to wear outrageous earrings and hair ornaments that she makes herself. Claud is Japanese-American and has beautiful dark almond-shaped eyes and perfect skin, which is amazing to me because she's an absolute junk food addict. I'm not kidding. She adores Ring Dings, candy kisses, and Mallomars. Her idea of a good lunch is a chocolate bar with peanuts and a can of fruit punch.

Then there's Kristy. When it comes to fashion she couldn't care less. First of all, Kristy is a full-fledged tomboy. She likes sports and even coaches a softball team called Kristy's Krushers. She has dark brown chin-length hair that she sometimes tucks under a baseball cap. And most days, like today, she wears her standard uniform — a turtleneck, jeans, and sneakers.

I waved to Kristy and Claud and then hurried across the crowded lunch room to join them.

"Guess what?" I announced as I placed my lunch next to Claudia's. "I'm going to save the planet."

Claudia just blinked her dark eyes at me and said, "It's about time."

Kristy took a big bite of her (ick) hamburger and cracked, "I *was* going to save it but I have a big softball game this afternoon."

"You two think you're so funny." I swatted at Kristy, who was grinning at me from across the table. "But I mean it. This grade period we're studying ecology in Mrs. Gonzalez's science class. She's asked us to come up with an independent project — "

"To save the earth," a voice finished from behind me. It was Stacey McGill, balancing a carton of yogurt and a small salad on her tray. She slipped into the seat beside Kristy. "I've got to do the same project. We only have a week to think of something, and so far my mind is a total blank."

Stacey is absolutely gorgeous, with fluffy blonde hair and these huge blue eyes with dark eyelashes. She's also very thin, which is partly caused by the strict diet she is on. You see, Stacey is diabetic, which means her body can't process sugar. She has to give herself insulin shots (ew) every day! I could never do that in a million years. Besides being a real knock-out, Stacey is very smart and ultra sophisticated. She used to live in New York City, but she and her mom moved to Stoneybrook when her parents got divorced. She still visits the city a lot to see her dad. In fact, sometimes she's on the train so much she says she feels like a commuter daughter.

Of all of us, I'd say Stacey is the coolest dresser. Today she was wearing floral leggings, a pink shirt with big sleeves, and a long vest covered in antique pins. A black fedora with a red cloth rose was perched on top of her shoulder length hair.

"Don't worry, Stacey," Claud said. "You'll

think of something. You're a whiz at math so science should be just as easy."

"Not true," Stacey said, taking a bite of a carrot stick. "They are two totally different subjects."

"Not to me," Claud added. "They both make me crazy. They both involve numbers and words you can't pronounce and things you have to memorize."

"Don't even mention memorizing," Mary Anne complained as she and her boyfriend, Logan, joined us at the table. "I think I just bombed a spelling test in English."

"Bombed," Logan repeated in his soft southern accent. (He's from Kentucky.) "Yeah, right. Mary Anne considers missing one question bombing a test."

Mary Anne poked Logan in the ribs with her elbow and he clutched his side and howled, "Ow! She got me!"

My friends spent the rest of the lunch hour talking about tests and classes, how disgusting the hot lunch was (Claudia called it "The Green Slime"), and what movie everyone wanted to see on the weekend. But I couldn't take my mind off the science project.

I thought about it for the rest of the school day and for my entire walk home. Usually Mary Anne walks with me, but she was scheduled to baby-sit for the Perkins girls.

10

When I reached my house I headed straight for my room, deciding to make a list of ideas for Mrs. Gonzalez's class. List-making always helps me decide about important issues. I've used it to decide who I'm going to invite to a dance or what outfit I'm going to wear for the first day of school or which homework assignment I'm going to do first.

I got out a pad and grabbed a black magic marker from my desk. Then I wrote in big bold letters this question:

HOW CAN I SAVE THE PLANET?

CHAPTER 2

Our kitchen clock read 5:20. I had only ten minutes to get to Claudia Kishi's house. I could just make it if I pedaled my bike really fast.

BSC meetings start promptly at 5:30. Kristy, who's club president, is really strict about that. She hates for anyone to be even one minute late. Kristy is president partly because the club was her idea and partly because she's a natural leader.

Kristy is also great with little kids. That's probably because she's had to be very responsible from an early age. Her dad just walked out one day when she was little and left Mrs. Thomas to raise four kids. Kristy has two older brothers and a younger brother. It was pretty hard on Mrs. Thomas until she met Watson Brewer, who is — are you ready for this? — a millionaire! Kristy's mom married Watson right after Kristy finished seventh grade. Now they live in this absolutely gorgeous mansion across town.

It's a good thing Kristy likes kids, because Watson has two little ones, a boy and a girl, from a previous marriage (they live with their father every other weekend, on some holidays, and for two weeks in the summer). Then Watson and Kristy's mom decided to adopt a little girl from Vietnam. Emily Michelle is two-and-a-half and a total doll. Luckily, Nannie, Kristy's grandmother, moved in to help with all those kids. On some weekends ten people live at her house. Can you imagine? I guess it's a good thing they live in that mansion.

Claudia Kishi is vice-president of the BSC. We hold our meetings at her house since she has her own phone and her own phone number. That's very important because from 5:30 to 6:00 every Monday, Wednesday, and Friday we need to have that line open to take calls from our clients.

I already told you that Claud is a really cool dresser. I'm sure it's because she's such a great artist. Besides being able to draw, she makes her own earrings, tie-dyes her own clothes, and designs these really neat belts and hair ornaments.

Claud is smart, too, but she's a terrible student. And the worst speller on the planet. Which is strange since her sister, Janine, is a full-fledged genius. Her parents are always pushing Claud to study harder and read good books (Claud has to hide her Nancy Drews along with her junk food) but I think they're proud of her artwork.

Mary Anne is our secretary. She keeps the club record book where we list clients' addresses, their phone numbers, and pertinent facts about their kids (like if one of them is allergic to milk, or has to be taken to piano lessons on Thursdays, or whatever). Mary Anne also uses the record book to assign each of us our jobs. Things can get pretty crazy trying to arrange baby-sitting jobs around our schedules. Jessi has dance lessons, Mal has orthodontist appointments, Kristy has softball practice, and Mary Anne has to remember all that. But she has never made a mistake.

Our treasurer is Stacey because she's an absolute math whiz. For awhile, when Stacey was gone, I handled the job. You see, I'm the alternate officer in the club. That means if anyone gets sick or moves, I take over her job. Boy, was I glad to see Stacey return to Stoneybrook because, let's face it, math is not one of my strengths.

The BSC also has two junior members. We call them "junior" because Mallory Pike and Jessica Ramsey are eleven (the rest of us are thirteen). They're not allowed to baby-sit at night, unless it's for their own families, so they take a lot of the afternoon and weekend jobs.

Mal and Jessi are best friends and alike in many ways. First of all, they are complete nuts when it comes to horses. Also, they both love to read and are the oldest kids in their families.

But they are also very different. Mal has *seven* brothers and sisters. When Mr. and Mrs. Pike go out, they hire two sitters.

Jessi, on the other hand, only has one sister, Becca and one brother, Squirt. (His real name is John Philip Ramsey, Jr., but that's a big name for such a little guy so the nurses at the hospital where he was born nicknamed him Squirt.)

Mal wants to be a writer and illustrator of children's books when she grows up. Jessi would like to be a ballerina. She's a wonderful dancer and has already performed in several professional productions. And Jessi is black and Mal is white, but that doesn't matter to them or anyone in the BSC.

Besides the five officers and two junior members, the BSC also has two associate members: Shannon Kilbourne and Mary Anne's boyfriend, Logan Bruno. They don't come to meetings but we call them if we have too many baby-sitting jobs and need a back-up.

So that's our club. Now I'll tell you how it

works. We meet, as I said, three days a week at Claud's house. If a client needs a sitter, he (or she) knows to call us during our meetings. This is great because all he has to do is dial one number to reach seven experienced sitters. Usually, one of us is available, and if not, we contact our associates.

While we wait for the phone to ring (and on some days it never stops!) we hold our club meeting.

Our president Kristy always sits in Claud's director's chair with a visor on her head and a pencil tucked behind one ear. She waits until the digital clock on Claudia's desk turns from 5:29 to 5:30, and then she calls the meeting to order.

Mondays are Dues Days and that's when Stacey collects our money. The dues pay for Claudia's phone bill and for Kristy's older brother, Charlie, to chauffeur her across town. (She used to live right across the street but Watson's mansion is on the other side of Stoneybrook.) We also use the money to buy supplies for our Kid-Kits.

Kid-Kits were one of Kristy's great ideas. We each got a box and decorated it, then filled it with old toys from our houses, and other things, such as books, stickers, scissors, and glue. The kids love them. I try to vary the things in my kit. You know, one week I'll bring

16

puppets, another week Play-Doh. And when we run out of crayons or coloring books, Stacey gives us money to restock our Kid-Kits.

After Stacey has doled out the money and *if* there's any left over, we sometimes splurge on a pizza party or a trip to the movies.

Another of Kristy's great ideas was the BSC notebook. It's kind of like a diary in which each of us writes down our sitting experiences. Writing in it can be a pain, but we agree that the notebook is really useful. It lets us know what's happening in the lives of the families we take care of — if one of the kids is having trouble adjusting to a new baby, or the parents are going through a divorce. This way we can be prepared.

So that's our club and how it works. Since today was Monday, I knew we would be busy. I pedaled as fast as I could to Claud's house, raced through her front door and collapsed on her bed just as the clock turned from 5:29 to 5:30.

Kristy raised an eyebrow at the sight of me gasping for air but since I was on time she really couldn't say anything. Instead she adjusted her visor and declared, "This meeting of the BSC is officially called to order. As you know, today is Dues Day."

Jessi joked, "I think we should all chip in to pay for an oxygen tank for Dawn."

17

I put one hand over my heart and said dramatically, "If I die now, please tell the world I died happy because I was on time to the Baby-sitter's Club meeting."

Everyone cracked up. Kristy swatted at me with her hand but before she could say anything the phone rang. I settled back between Mary Anne and Claud as Claud picked up the phone.

"Hello, Baby-sitter's Club. *Your* kids are *our* business." (Kristy gave Claudia a look. She likes us all to act very professional.)

"Oh, hello, Mrs. Barrett," Claudia said as she tried to saw off the top of a huge bag of Gummi bears with a letter opener. She'd stashed the candy in the lower drawer of her desk so her parents wouldn't see it. "Tomorrow afternoon? Great. I'll call you right back." Claud hung up the phone. "She needs a sitter tomorrow," she announced.

Mary Anne checked the record book. Mal and Jessi already had jobs and Stacey had a doctor's appointment. "Claud has an art lesson and I promised Logan I'd go the mall with him," Mary Anne said. "So it's either Dawn or Kristy."

"You live much closer to the Barretts," Kristy said to me. "Why don't you take it?"

"Sure." The Barrett kids, who I used to refer

to as the Impossible Three, were now some of my favorites. I was glad to take the job.

For the next twenty minutes the phone did not stop ringing. Mal booked a job with the Arnold twins on Wednesday, Claud with the Hobarts Tuesday night, and Jessi with the Johanssens on Wednesday afternoon.

Stacey had just finished collecting everyone's dues when the meeting was over. I had hoped to discuss my list of ideas for my science project with the club, but realized I'd have to wait till the next day.

That was okay, because the really great idea didn't come to me until I baby-sat for the Barretts.

CHAPTER 3

*W*oof! Woof!

Pow, the Barretts' basset hound, met me on their front porch when I arrived to baby-sit on Tuesday. He was wearing a baby bonnet, and a plastic bottle was tied around his collar. He looked miserable.

"Come here, you bad dog," five-year-old Suzi Barrett cried as she ran around the side of the house. "You're supposed to take your nap now."

"Hi, Suzi," I said, kneeling down to hug her. "Is Pow giving you trouble?"

Suzi nodded. "I'm playing house and he's my baby."

Then the front door flew open and Buddy Barrett, wearing a cowboy hat and chaps, shouted, "Hooray, it's Dawn!" He flung a loop of clothesline around my shoulders and shouted, "Got you!"

20

"Oh, no!" I cried, pretending to be scared. "What's going on?"

"I'm the sheriff," Buddy declared. "And you're under arrest."

"No, she's not." Suzi put her hands on her hips and faced her brother. "Dawn is going to play house with me and Pow."

"Dawn! Dawn!" another voice shouted from inside the house.

Marnie, the two-year-old, who has curly blonde hair and big blue eyes, raced down the stairs and through the front door and wrapped her arms around my knees.

I bent down and picked her up. "It's a good thing you showed up, Marnie," I said. "I think you broke up the argument Sheriff Buddy and Mother Suzi were about to have."

When I first met the three Barrett kids they were impossible. Their hair was uncombed, their house was a total mess, and they acted pretty wild. But I soon discovered it was only because their parents were going through a rough divorce and Mrs. Barrett was having trouble getting a job and running the house at the same time. Things are much better now. The house isn't quite so messy, Mrs. Barrett has a part-time job, and the divorce isn't as awful as it was at first. The Barrett kids can still be rowdy, but they're a lot of fun.

Mrs. Barrett appeared in the front hallway,

looking as if she had just stepped off the cover of some fashion magazine. I'm not kidding, she was absolutely gorgeous.

"Oh, hello, Dawn. I'm glad you're here," she said. "The kids have been looking forward to seeing you all day."

I smiled at her and then ruffled Buddy's hair. "I've been looking forward to seeing them, too." I held up my Kid-Kit. "I've got a surprise I want to show them."

"Oooh, I want to see!" Suzi shouted, hopping up and down.

"Me, first," Buddy cried.

"Me, me," Marnie chimed in.

"Let's go into the living room and I'll show all three of you," I said.

Mrs. Barrett slipped on a light jacket that she'd taken from the hall closet. "I'll be at the dentist's office. I've written her name and number on the pad by the phone. I'll be back in about two hours," she told me. "There are crackers and some cans of juice on the kitchen counter. 'Bye, kids!'"

Buddy and Suzi waved good-bye but didn't look up. They were too preoccupied with what was in my Kid-Kit. I said good-bye to Mrs. Barrett and then carried Marnie into the living room. We sat in a circle around the box.

Buddy pulled out the paper bag holding my

surprise and peeked inside. His face fell when he saw what it was. "It's a book."

"But not just any book," I said mysteriously. "Open it up and tell me what you see."

Suzi pulled back the cover and then squealed with delight. "Stickers! I love stickers."

Buddy tried to sound out the words written across the top of the big vinyl-coated page. "Mah-reen. Werrrrld." He looked up at me with a grin and repeated it. "Marine World."

"That's right, Buddy," I said. "Good job."

The book was actually a fold-out map of Marine World. It showed several ponds, a walkway, waterfalls, and slides. In the middle of the fold-out was a piece of paper covered in stickers.

"What kind of animals do you see there?" I asked them.

Suzi peeled the stickers off the page, calling them by name. "Fish. Whale. Seal. Hippo-lot-a-mess."

I couldn't help giggling. "I think you mean, hippo-*pot*-a-*mus*."

Suzi nodded solemnly. "That's what I said."

"Dawn." Buddy held up a sticker. "What kind of fish is this?"

"It's a dolphin. They're one of the smartest creatures in the ocean."

"You mean, they can do tricks?" Suzi asked.

"Yes, but they also communicate with each other and with us. In dolphin language, of course."

"I want one," Buddy declared.

"Where would you keep it?" I asked.

"In the bathtub," Suzi suggested.

"Oh, a dolphin's much bigger than that," I replied. "And it needs lots of room to swim in. Here's something sad about dolphins. Did you know that a lot of them die just because we like to eat tuna fish?"

Buddy looked at me skeptically. "What's tuna fish got to do with dolphins?"

"Well, some fishing fleets use nets that accidentally trap millions of dolphins every year. And the sad thing is that the fishermen could catch the tuna without using nets, but they don't want to."

"How come?" Buddy demanded.

"They say it's too expensive that way."

"That's not fair," he protested.

"How do you know all of this?" Suzi asked, cupping the sticker gently in her hand.

"I've been studying our planet and the animals that live on it in school." I pointed to the Marine World sticker book. "That's why I bought this book. Half of the money I spent on it will go to the Save the Dolphins fund."

Buddy leapt to his feet. "I want to save the dolphins."

"So do I," Suzi said, joining him.

"Me, too!" Marnie sprang to her feet and grabbed Suzi's hand. The three kids hopped up and down chanting, "Save the dolphins." (It sounded a lot like, "Save the doll's fins.")

"You can save them," I said, excitedly.

They quieted down and Suzi asked, "We can? How?"

"Well, first of all, we can write the tuna companies and tell them we won't buy their tuna if they keep hurting the dolphins," I explained. "Look, I'll write the letters and you guys can sign them."

"Yea!" Suzi squealed so loudly that Pow started barking. The baby bonnet had fallen over his eyes and, as he barked, he struggled to knock it off his nose with one of his big paws.

I pulled the bonnet off Pow's face and held up my hands to quiet Suzi. "There are a lot of other things we can do, too — things that will help all of the animals in the sea."

"Like what?" Buddy asked.

I'd checked out several books from the library about ecology and our planet and had looked through them during lunch, so the ideas were still fresh in my mind. "Well, we can start by making sure the garbage we dump in the ocean doesn't hurt the fish and animals."

"I never throw my garbage in the ocean," Suzi said, putting her fists on her hips and looking indignant. "That's littering."

I couldn't resist giving her a hug. "I know you don't, but some big companies do. Come on." I took her hand. "Let's go in the kitchen and I'll show you what gets thrown in the water."

Buddy, Marnie, and Suzi trotted obediently after me. Our first stop was the kitchen counter. A six-pack of soda sat by the telephone. I pointed to the plastic rings holding the cans together. "These are really dangerous to fish and sea animals. When they float in the water, they look like food. Then sea turtles swallow them, which is harmful to their insides. Seals and birds, like pelicans and seagulls, get them caught around their necks. Even fish can get tangled in them."

"But what can we do about it?" Buddy asked earnestly.

I opened the top drawer by the sink and pulled out a pair of scissors. "Clip the rings so there are no circles for animals to get caught on."

"I want to do it!" Suzi cried, reaching for the scissors.

"No, I do," Buddy said stubbornly.

I realized I had to think fast and find Suzi another chore. I looked around the room for an idea and spied the garbage can.

"Suzi, why don't you look in the garbage and pull out every can you find?" I unfolded a paper bag that had been tucked between the refrigerator and the wall. "Put them in here and we'll recycle the aluminum."

"We're going to take it for a tricycle ride?" Suzi asked, squinting one eye shut.

I couldn't help laughing. "No. Recycle means to use things over and over again." I pulled an empty can of juice out of the trash. "If we don't throw this away, it can go back to the factory and be used again and again. But if we toss it out, then it floats around our oceans, hurting all those innocent sea creatures."

Suzi dove for the trash basket. "I'm going to make sure every single can is re-tricycled."

"Good for you!" I couldn't believe how much fun it was to teach the Barretts about ecology. We spent the remainder of the afternoon talking about ways we could save our planet, and the animals on it.

"Turn off dripping faucets," I said, pointing to the leaky kitchen faucet. "That will save water."

Mrs. Barrett had made some cream cheese-and-nut sandwiches and put them in plastic bags.

"Don't throw away these bags," I said. "Recycle them. We'll wash them out and let them dry. Then your mom can use them again."

Buddy and Suzi and even Marnie were such eager students that suddenly I got this idea. If the Barrett kids were this anxious to learn about ecology, maybe other kids in the neighborhood would be, too. What if I taught an after-school ecology class to the kids I babysat for? It would be the perfect project for Mrs. Gonzalez's class and, best of all, it would be fun!

After I left the Barretts that afternoon, I couldn't stop thinking about my project. I knew that getting all the kids to one location and teaching the class would be a lot of work. I also realized I would need help. After dinner that night, I dialed Stacey and told her about my great idea.

"Kids, of all people, should know how to save the planet," I said to Stacey on the phone. "After all, it's going to be theirs the longest."

"Dawn, it's a terrific idea," Stacey agreed. "And I found the perfect book that will be just right for this class. It's called *50 Simple Things Kids Can Do to Save the Earth*."

"I think I've seen that at the library," I said, making a note of the title on the pad of paper by the phone. "Great! So we have our textbook and our project, and it's only Tuesday. We're way ahead of the rest of the class."

"There's only one problem," Stacey said. "Do you think Mrs. Gonzalez will let us work on the project together? I mean, we're not even in the same class."

That thought had occurred to me but I figured, since it was such a great idea, Mrs. Gonzalez would go for it. She'd just have to.

"I'll talk to her first thing tomorrow morning," I said, trying to sound confident. "Just bring the book and start thinking of how we're going to put this project together."

CHAPTER 4

"She said yes!"

My voice echoed down the hallway at Stoneybrook Middle School as I shouted to Stacey across the crowd of students milling around their lockers. Several of them turned to stare at me. Normally I might have been embarrassed but not today. Today I didn't care.

Mrs. Gonzalez had taken the afternoon to think about the project. After school she had called me into her classroom for a talk. "I think it's a wonderful idea," she'd said. "You and Stacey just need to keep clear records of who contributes what to the project."

Stacey, who had been more worried than me, let out a squeal of delight at my news. "All right!" Then she gave me a big hug.

I caught Brent Jensen nudging his friend Todd Long and pointing at us, a smirk on his face. Stacey stuck her tongue out at him and

30

I said, "Take a picture, it'll last longer."

Then we raced out of the big glass doors of SMS into the open air.

"We have to get started right away," I said as we hurried down the sidewalk. "We have to make lists, and decide on what day of the week we should hold our classes."

Stacey nodded. "That means a ton of phone calls. Why don't you come to my house? We can use the phone in my room."

Stacey isn't like Claud, who actually has her own telephone *number*, but she does have her own extension, which I think is very cool.

We hurried to Stacey's house, which is this hundred-year-old house directly behind Mallory's house. We tossed our school books onto the living room couch and then I followed Stacey into the kitchen.

"As I see it," Stacey said as she made us a healthy after-school snack of celery and carrot sticks, "we should schedule six weeks worth of lessons."

I took a loud crunchy bite of celery. "Each week we could deal with one or two different ways of saving the planet. Week one could focus on recycling."

Stacey nodded. "Week two — conserving water. Then maybe ways to save energy."

"Right."

She poured us each a tall glass of juice and

we carried our snacks to her room. I sat cross-legged on her bed, cradling the plate of celery and carrot sticks on my lap.

"We could follow the rest of the headings from Mrs. Gonzalez's class." I ticked them off on my fingers. "Acid Rain, Air Pollution, Vanishing Animal Life, Too Much Garbage, and Water Pollution. And then the last week we could concentrate on getting the word out to others."

"You mean, like having the kids call people up?" Stacey asked.

"They could do that or . . ." I squinted one eye shut to think. "How about if we do something like invite people to come to a fair? With exhibits and posters — "

"That the kids made themselves," Stacey chimed in.

I snapped my fingers. "We could call it a Green Fair."

"Dawn, that's a fabulous idea!" Stacey said excitedly.

"I think we're definitely on the right track," I declared.

"This project will be the best one in the whole school," Stacey agreed.

"It will be," I said slowly, "*if* we can get some kids to attend our classes."

"There's no time to waste," Stacey said,

picking up the phone. "Let's start calling people."

"Wait!" I pulled my yellow notepad out of my bookbag. "Let's make a list of people to call, and what we want to tell them. Then we should include that list in our report."

"That's good." Stacey searched for a pen in the top drawer of her desk. "That way Mrs. Gonzalez can see all the work we've put into the project."

I took the cap off my special black ink pen and started to write. "First we'll dial our BSC clients and ask if their kids are interested in taking our class."

Stacey crossed her fingers. "And hopefully the kids will be so excited about the idea that they'll all sign up."

"Then we'll find out what days are free for them," I continued.

"Terrific." Stacey held her dialing finger over the phone buttons. "Who should I start with?"

"Try Kristy's house," I suggested. "We can tell her about the idea and see if David Michael is interested."

While Stacey dialed, I listed the names of several of our clients in my notebook. Then I drew a line across the top and wrote down the days of the week. I figured I'd put an x on the days the kids were available. Then we'd be able to decide which day we should hold our class.

"Kristy? It's me, Stacey. Dawn and I are working on the best idea in the world." Stacey paused for a second and then rolled her eyes at me. "Okay, the *second* best idea in the world. The BSC *was* the best idea."

I giggled and put my ear beside the receiver to hear the rest of their conversation. Stacey explained about the project for Mrs. Gonzalez's class to Kristy.

"So what I want to know is," Stacey finished, "do you think David Michael would like to attend?"

"Of course he would," Kristy said enthusiastically. "But he's not home right now. Tell me where it's going to be. I'll ask him about it."

"Where's it going to be?" Stacey's eyes suddenly widened. "Gee. Dawn and I hadn't even thought about that. Hold on a second."

Stacey put her hand over the mouthpiece and the two of us held a hasty conference. "Do you want it to be at your house?" she asked.

I shook my head. "I think it should be at your house because you're more centrally located."

"Good idea." Stacey spoke into the phone

once more. "Kristy, we're going to hold the classes at my house. I'm sure my mom won't mind. We haven't decided on a date yet, but we wanted to find out what days were best for the kids."

"Wednesdays or Thursdays are best for David Michael," Kristy replied.

I was still listening at the receiver. Now I marked two Xs on my new chart.

Then Kristy threw us for another loop. "How will he get to the class and home again?" she asked.

Stacey's eyes, which had grown big before, were now huge. "Uh, just a sec and I'll talk to Dawn." She covered the receiver with her hand and whispered, "How are the kids going to get to my house? David Michael lives all the way across town."

I looked down at the chart for a moment, and then said, "Let me talk to Kristy." Stacey handed me the phone and I said, "Hi, Kristy, it's me. Listen, if we held the class on Wednesdays, David Michael could walk to Stacey's with us after school and then ride back with you after the BSC meeting."

"What would he do during our meeting?" Kristy asked logically.

"Maybe he could wait in the Kishis' living room," I suggested. "Or maybe we could ask someone else to take him home earlier."

I must have sounded pretty uncertain because Kristy promptly said, "Look, why don't you guys work out some of the details and call us back later. By that time David Michael should be home."

"Okay. 'Bye." I hung up the phone and gasped, "Boy, do I feel stupid. We started making our calls without working out important details like where the classes are going to be."

Stacey looked as embarrassed as I felt. "It's a good thing we called Kristy first. Otherwise the parents would have thought we were real airheads."

I looked at my notepad once again. "Is there anything else we forgot?"

"Well, we never did decide how long the class would be," Stacey said, studying my list.

"I think it should be an hour. From 3:30 to 4:30. Any longer and the kids will get restless."

We agreed to find out who would need transportation. "That way we can make a list and then maybe ask your mom or mine to help carpool," I finished.

After only an hour of dialing clients, we found eleven members for our class: Charlotte Johanssen, Becca Ramsey, David Michael Thomas, Karen and Andrew Brewer, Buddy and Suzi Barrett, Nicky and Vanessa Pike, and

Hannie and Linny Papadakis. And because the Papadakises live across the street from David Michael, Mrs. Papadakis offered to drive the kids who needed a ride to the classes. Things were working out perfectly.

Stacey checked the list and said, "Only one more family to call, the Kormans. Do you want to do it?"

"Sure." I dialed quickly and when Mrs. Korman answered, I started my speech. By now I'd said it so many times I was feeling like a real pro.

"Hi, Mrs. Korman, this is Dawn Schafer. Stacey McGill and I are going to be teaching an ecology class one day a week after school. This class will last an hour and is aimed at elementary school age children. Stacey and I are doing it as a project for our school but we feel very strongly that you're never too young to start protecting our planet. It's important for everyone to know that we *can* make a difference."

As I spoke Stacey gave me a big smile. She was obviously impressed by my speech. I explained to Mrs. Korman about the six classes, and how they were absolutely free, and also about the Green Fair. I don't know what came over me but I added a new touch.

"Our Green Fair will serve two purposes," I declared. "It will help tell people about ecology and what's happening to the environment, and it will also be a way to raise money for an organization, which we will choose later, that helps save the planet."

Stacey whispered, "What a brilliant idea."

It was hard to stay calm during the rest of the conversation.

"We're very proud of our project, Mrs. Korman," I said, hoping my voice didn't sound too excited. "I'll call you back and let you know the exact date and time of the class by tomorrow afternoon."

I hung up the phone and announced, "Well, that does it. Thirteen kids for our class."

"Lucky thirteen," Stacey giggled. "I love it that the Green Fair will also be a fundraiser for an environmental organization."

I grinned. "If our project goes right, we'll be showing not just our school but all of Stoneybrook that we are concerned enough about our community to do something to change it."

"All right, Dawn!" Stacey applauded enthusiastically and I hopped off the bed and took a bow. If this was how our project was going to go, I couldn't wait for it to get started.

CHAPTER 5

"The first meeting of the Save the Planet class is officially called to order," Stacey announced to the thirteen children sitting cross-legged on her living room floor.

"Yea!" Buddy Barrett led the applause. I knew we could count on him to be an enthusiastic student.

After calling roll, Stacey gestured to me and said, "Dawn will pass out the special badges we want you to wear during our classes."

Stacey and I had spent an hour cutting out cardboard circles at her house. Then we used glitter ink to write the words KIDS CARE on them.

"These will be a constant reminder to ourselves and to our parents," she told the kids, "that what we are doing is important."

After Stacey and I finished pinning the badges on the kids, I stepped back up to the front of the group. All of a sudden I felt a little nervous. I'd never actually taught a class before. I looked down at my notebook, where Stacey and I had carefully plotted out every second of the class. "First, I want to ask you a question," I began. "Do you think our world is clean?"

Becca Ramsey waved her hand frantically in the air.

Stacey grinned. "Becca?"

Becca, who is eight and a half, stood up and said, very seriously, "Yes, except where there is dirt, like under our lawn or at the park."

It was hard not to giggle at her reply but Stacey and I managed to keep a straight face. Then nine-year-old Bill Korman said, "It's clean when it rains and everything gets washed."

Charlotte Johanssen, whose mother is a doctor, raised her hand. "But the world is not always clean. Sometimes the air gets dirty from the smoke that comes out of factories and cars."

"That's right," I said. "Our world may look clean and shiny, like after a rainfall, but things float around in the air that make it very dirty. And it's not just dirt like the kind you find under your lawn. This dirt can come in all shapes and sizes."

"Like trash on the side of the road," Stacey chimed in.

"Or it can appear in water," I added. "Have any of you ever seen a shiny film on the water in a creek?"

Linny Papadakis nodded vigorously. "I have. And sometimes I've even seen this foam that looks like bubble bath floating on the top of it."

Stacey and I exchanged concerned looks. "The shiny film is oil that shouldn't be there," I explained. "And the foam is probably soap coming from homes or factories. They're both bad for the water and the fish that try to live in the water. It's like poison to them."

"Oh, no!" Becca Ramsey gasped in alarm.

"This dirt is called pollution," Stacey said. "Can everyone say it?"

"*Plushun!*" Andrew Brewer called out.

"*Po-lu-ton*," Suzi Barrett said, giggling.

Stacey and I smiled at each other. Even if they couldn't pronounce the word, the kids seemed very enthusiastic about what could have been a boring subject.

"Pollution comes in all kinds of forms," I continued. "Sometimes it's invisible. Does anybody know what that means?"

Vanessa raised her hand. "Invisible means you can't see it. Like ghosts."

"Ghosts!"

This set off a rumbling among the younger members of the group, especially Andrew, who is only four. He looked over his shoulder and muttered, "I don't like ghosts."

I hurried to get them back on track. "This pollution isn't a ghost but it can be scary. It's scary because it hurts things."

Stacey nodded. "It gets in the water we drink. It gets in the air we breathe and makes us cough. It even goes way up in the sky and tears a hole in a special layer of gas called ozone that circles the earth. The ozone protects us from the hot, hot rays of the sun."

"You mean, we could get sunburned without it?" Hannie Papadakis asked, wide-eyed.

"That's right," I replied. "We could get sunburned, and so would everything on the planet. And if the ozone layer disappears, we'll just get hotter and hotter."

"That's terrible," Vanessa Pike murmured.

"It *is* terrible," I agreed. "But this class is going to teach you ways to stop that from happening."

"We're going to teach you ways to save the animals, the water, the air, and the ozone layer," Stacey said.

"And we're going to tell you what to do with the trash you find along the side of the road," I added.

"I know what to do with that," Nicky Pike said, rolling his eyes. "You throw it away."

"That's *one* way to help clean up the earth,"

42

Stacey said. "But we've found an even better thing to do with that trash."

I pointed to our first poster and read the title out loud. "Recycle."

"Hey, I know what that means." Buddy hopped up from where he was sitting and joined Stacey and me at the front of the living room. "Recycling means reusing things." Then he turned to me and whispered, "Right?"

"Right," I whispered back.

Stacey pointed to a drawing she'd made on the poster. It showed the earth covered in a huge mound of garbage. "If we just keep throwing things away, our garbage dumps will get so huge there won't be any room for us to move. The garbage could take over the planet."

I held up a collage I had made of things that can be recycled. I'd cut pictures out of magazines and glued them on poster board. It wasn't as artistically designed as if Claudia had made it but I think it was okay.

"Some things can be used over and over again," I said, "like glass and aluminum cans and paper. So instead of throwing them away — what should we do?"

All of the kids shouted, *"Recycle them*!" (They were getting into the shouting part of the class.)

"Right," Stacey agreed. "Now, how many things can you name that are made of glass?"

"Bottles!" Nicky Pike called out.

"Good," I said. "What else?"

The kids shouted out their answers all at once. "Mirrors! TVs! Plates! Windows! Windshields! Light bulbs! Eyeglasses! Computer screens!" The list seemed endless.

"Did you know," Stacey began after everyone had quieted down, "we throw away twenty-eight *billion* bottles and jars each year?"

"Is that a lot?" Andrew Brewer asked.

"It's more than you could ever count." I chuckled.

Vanessa raised her hand. "But where are we supposed to recycle our bottles?"

Stacey and I exchanged looks. We only knew of one place and that was not nearby.

"Right now Stoneybrook has just one recycling center, down near the courthouse," I explained. "But it's kind of far for us to walk to. Your parents will have to drive you there."

"What if they can't?" Suzi Barrett asked.

I paused. "That's a good question, Suzi. Stacey and I will have to work on that."

I made a note in my book to find out why there weren't more recycling centers in Stoneybrook. Meanwhile Stacey explained our first project to the group.

"Okay, kids," she said. "Today we're going

to dig a hole in my backyard and bury some — "

"Treasures?" David Michael asked, excitedly.

Stacey laughed. "Some of the things we bury will turn out to be treasures. The other stuff won't. Follow me."

The kids scrambled into the McGills' kitchen where Stacey and I had set our supplies on the kitchen counter.

"What do you see here?" Stacey asked the group.

Charlotte wrinkled her nose. "An apple core, one that's already turning brown."

Stacey nodded. "What else?"

"Some bunny food," Suzi Barrett said, pointing at a leaf of lettuce.

"That's correct," Stacey said, laughing. "And?"

"An old cup," Bill Korman said.

"But that's not just any kind of cup," I said, joining the group in the kitchen. "That cup is made of Styrofoam."

"That's the stuff that squeaks when you bite into it," Linny Papadakis pointed out.

Just thinking about squeaking Styrofoam sent shivers down my spine. "And what is this last item?" I asked.

"Garbage," Becca Ramsey said, holding up the wrapping from a box of cookies.

"That's right," I said. "This is plastic."

"Now we're all going to go outside and bury these," Stacey said.

Melody Korman raised her hand. "But why?"

"Because we're going to find out which items are biodegradable," I replied. Blank stares followed that announcement, so I quickly explained, "That means they'll dissolve back into the earth and become good garbage. The things that aren't biodegradable will just sit there."

"So we're going to bury these four items," Stacey continued, "and then in a couple of weeks we'll dig them up and see which ones are still there."

"All right, here's a shovel," Buddy Barrett cried, grabbing the gardening trowel lying on the kitchen counter. "I want to carry it."

"No." Nicky Pike grabbed for it. "I want to."

"Let me!" Karen Brewer hopped up and down, waving her hand in my face.

Suddenly, everyone in the room was shouting at once. For a second I was certain we'd never calm them down. Thinking fast, Stacey grabbed a whistle from a junk drawer in the kitchen and blew on it hard.

Tweet!

Everyone froze in place.

"In order for us to save the planet," she said in a very calm voice, "we have to work together. That means taking turns."

I did some quick arithmetic in my head, then made the assignments. "Buddy, Charlotte, Becca, David Michael, and Melody will carry these items to the backyard." The five kids cheered but fell silent when they saw Stacey get ready to blow her whistle again. "Then Linny, Bill, Nicky, and Vanessa will dig the holes."

The four kids beamed at each other.

"And then," I went on, "Hannie, Suzi, Karen, and Andrew will bury the items."

There were big smiles all around the room. Stacey and I gave each other quick looks of relief.

We marched the kids into the garden and each one performed his job. When the last bit of dug-up dirt had been placed on the last hole, the kids packed it down with their feet. It was really cute. (I think stomping the dirt was their favorite part of the whole class.)

Finally Stacey placed labels attached to garden stakes over each spot. *Lettuce*, *Plastic*, *Apple*, and *Styrofoam*. The kids stood by, proudly admiring their handiwork.

"All right, everybody," I said, "that's it for our first class. Stay tuned for next week when we'll become water leak detectives and start planning our Green Fair."

"Green fairies?" Suzi Barrett repeated.

"No." I chuckled. "Fair. Green Fair. Which is kind of an ecology carnival."

"You mean, like a talent show, with animal acts?" Becca sounded excited. Once she entered a pet show, and her hamster, Misty, had won best all-around pet.

"Let me try," Stacey whispered. She clasped her hands in front of her and said, "Each week we'll do a different experiment. At the end of six weeks, we'll put on a Green Fair, with booths to display the results of our experiments, and also to teach our neighbors what we've learned."

"In the meantime — " I pointed to our badges. "What do we tell our parents and friends?"

All the children shouted at once, "Kids *Care!*"

I checked my watch. Exactly one hour had gone by. Now it was time to return the kids to their homes, which was almost as complicated as planning the class. Mrs. Papadakis was going to take the Kormans, David Michael, and Hannie and Linny home. The Pike kids could just walk through Stacey's backyard to their house. Stacey and I would escort the others home.

I have to say, by the end of that day, I was totally exhausted. But it was a good kind of tired. I went to sleep that night feeling very proud that I, Dawn Schafer, was actually doing something to Save the Planet.

CHAPTER 6

It was almost time for another BSC meeting, and I couldn't wait. Boy, did I have some news to tell my friends! I had been on the phone all afternoon trying to find out about Stoneybrook's recycling program and I'd discovered that basically they didn't have one. Can you believe it? No wonder most of the kids in my class didn't know about recycling.

I was so anxious to talk to Stacey and everyone else that I reached Claud's house a full ten minutes ahead of time. She was in the kitchen wearing big cooking mitts on each hand.

"Come on in, Dawn." Claudia pointed to the oven. "I want to show you my latest design."

"You're making cookies?"

"No! Dough earrings." Claud pointed to the timer, which had less than a minute left on it. "They're almost done."

"Dough? You mean people can eat them?"

Claudia giggled and shook her head. "No. These are like dough ornaments that you hang on a Christmas tree. After I paint them I'm going to cover them with shellac."

Leave it to Claudia to think of something clever like that. Peering through the oven door, I could see little bits of dough shaped into dogs and cats. They were turning a golden brown.

Ding!

"Just in time," Claud said. "The meeting's about to start."

She pulled the cookie sheet out of the oven and set it on a metal rack on top of the stove. Then she turned to me and wiggled her eyebrows. "Now let's have a snack."

Claud reached into her refrigerator and handed me an apple. Then she dug in her backpack and pulled out an enormous bag of chocolate drops.

I was appalled. Not just by the huge bag of candy she was about to eat but by the way the candy had been packaged. "Look at that, Claud," I said. "Each candy is individually wrapped in plastic."

"Yeah." With a grin, Claudia tore off the wrapper and popped one in her mouth. "Isn't that great?"

"It's *terrible*," I said. "Do you know how

51

bad plastic is for the earth? That stuff will never dissolve."

She studied the next piece of candy. "Gee, I never thought about that."

"Well, it's time we all start thinking about it," I said sternly. "Next time, don't buy candy that's individually wrapped."

Claudia saluted and clicked her heels together. "Yes, ma'am."

"What's going on in here?" Kristy peeked in the kitchen. She gestured with her thumb at the ceiling. "We're supposed to be upstairs for our meeting, you know."

"I'm making art," Claudia replied, "and Dawn's giving me a lecture about garbage."

She and Kristy both laughed. Normally I would have joined them but, after spending the last few days worrying about pollution, I didn't find the subject very funny.

"Speaking of garbage," Kristy joked as we made our way to Claud's room, "did you see what they served for lunch today?"

Claud made a face. "Mystery Meat on a Taco Shell. It tasted awful."

"But what was worse," I added, "was the dessert. Fruit cocktail in Styrofoam cups. Do you know how terrible Styrofoam is for the environment?"

"No," Kristy said, winking at Claud, "but I have a feeling you're going to tell us."

52

I ignored her kidding and said, "Styrofoam is permanent garbage. It can never become part of the earth. I mean, five hundred years from now, those little cups that held the fruit cocktail will still be around."

"Ooh!" Kristy murmured to Claud. "Dawn sounds serious."

"I am," I said, sitting cross-legged on Claud's bed. "Ever since I started researching this project for Mrs. Gonzalez's class, my eyes have really been opened."

"So have mine," Mary Anne said as she entered the room. "Did you know that the Rodowskys' dog, can sing 'Home on the Range'?"

"Music and *words*?" Kristy cracked.

Mary Anne nudged Kristy with her elbow. "Of course not the words, but if you sing the melody, he'll join in. I found that out when I was baby-sitting this afternoon."

"That's amazing," Claud exclaimed. "The Rodowskys should have entered Bo when you and Dawn held that pet show."

Stacey, Mal, and Jessi hurried into Claud's room just as the numbers on the digital clock flipped over to 5:30. Mal and Jessi took their usual places on the floor and Stacey hopped up beside me on the bed as Kristy called the meeting to order.

While we waited for the phone to ring,

Kristy asked, "Does anyone have any announcements to make?"

Mallory cleared her throat. "I just thought everyone should know that the Ohdner kids have come down with the measles."

"Oh, no," everyone moaned.

"But!" Mal raised one hand. "I was the last to sit for them, and I've already had the measles, so I think it's okay."

Next Jessi spoke up. "Mary Anne, would you write in the schedule book that I can't sit for anyone on Monday, Wednesday, and Friday next week? Frederick Duvall from the New York City Ballet is teaching a special technique class on those days."

"You're kidding!" Stacey gasped. "Frederick Duvall? I've seen him dance." When Stacey lived with her parents in New York City, they used to go to the ballet all the time. "He's wonderful."

Jessi nodded excitedly. "I know. I'm already nervous about taking his class."

Mal patted her on the knee. "Don't worry. You'll be terrific. As usual."

I started to say something about recycling, but the phone rang. It was Mrs. Prezzioso, looking for a sitter for Friday night.

I guess my friends must have discussed who could take the job but I wasn't listening. I was too busy thinking about Stoneybrook's recycling problem and how I was going to fix it. Then I guess someone asked me a question because the next thing I knew, Stacey was waving her hand in front of my face.

"Earth to Dawn!" she said. "Are you in there?"

"What?" I blinked several times.

"I can take the job," Kristy said, "but if you want it, that's okay with me."

"What job?" I asked.

Claud, who was busy passing her bag of candy around the room, announced, "Dawn's got her mind on other things. Like permanent garbage."

"Sorry, Kristy," I said as everyone laughed at Claud's joke. "I wasn't paying attention. You take the job."

The phone rang two more times and Mal and Mary Anne each agreed to take an afternoon job. Then the room became quiet. I thought if I didn't speak up then, I'd never get to explain my idea.

"I have a very important announcement, everyone. I made a few calls today and discovered that Stoneybrook doesn't have a recycling program. They have that one bin by the courthouse, where people can bring their cans and bottles, but that's it. So I've decided to do something about it."

Kristy turned to Stacey. "Is this part of your science project?"

Stacey shrugged. "I don't think so. We're teaching that class."

"This is completely separate from our class assignment," I explained. "This is my own project. I want SMS to become a true recycling collection spot."

"For what?" Jessi asked.

"Everything!" I could feel my voice growing louder with excitement as I said, "Do you realize how many items can be recycled? Newspapers, computer papers, plastic bottles, glass bottles, jars, aluminum foil." I pointed to Claud's wastebasket, where an empty Coke can lay. "That can. You could redeem it and get a nickel."

"Oops!" Claud giggled. "I guess I was just being lazy."

"Do you realize we use over 65 billion aluminum cans a year?" I said. "And if everyone threw theirs away, like Claudia, that would be a monstrous amount of unnecessary garbage."

"Boy," Kristy said to Stacey under her breath. "Dawn's really serious."

"You're right," I said, folding my arms across my chest. "This is very important to me, and it should be to all of you."

"It is," Mary Anne said gently. "I guess

we're just not as upset about it as you are."

"Well, you should be." I pointed to Mary Anne's record book. "Look at the amount of paper you waste by writing on just one side of each sheet. Did you know that each of us uses five hundred and eighty pounds of paper a year? And it takes fifteen years for a tree to grow big enough to be made into paper. We're wasting a lot of time and trees."

Mary Anne stared down at the club record book, her cheeks a deep red. "Next time I promise to write on both sides of the paper, Dawn."

I realized I had embarrassed her and I felt bad about it. "Thanks, Mary Anne," I said, with an encouraging smile. "It means a lot to me. And next time we have to buy more paper for the club, I'd like to propose that we make sure it's recycled paper."

Kristy shrugged. "That's all right with me." She looked around the room at the rest of the club. "Any objections?"

Everyone shook their heads.

The next fifteen minutes were filled with phone calls, so we couldn't talk about my project anymore. Just before the meeting ended, Claud announced, "I want everyone to come into the kitchen and see the new jewelry I've made. There's something for each of you. And," she raised one finger, "Dawn will be glad to hear that my jewelry is completely biodegradable."

Everyone giggled but me. I knew that I was starting to sound like a grumpy old teacher, lecturing everyone, but I couldn't help it. If I couldn't convince the BSC of the importance of protecting our planet, how was I going to convince the town of Stoneybrook?

Saturday

Has everybody gone Green Crazy? Nothing's been the same at my house since Dawn and Stacey started their Save the Planet class.

Mal and I sat for the Pike kids on Saturday and were searched by The Green Meanies (that's what I called them)

My brothers and sisters made Jessi and me go on a complete inspection of the entire house looking for ways to Save the Planet.

Then we made lunch and were yelled at by practically every kid in the Pike family.

No offense, Dawn, but do you think your students may be going a little overboard?

59

It was Saturday morning and Jessi and Mal had been asked to sit for the Pike kids. Vanessa and Nicky are the only ones in my Save the Planet class but I guess they were so excited about ecology that they made everyone else in their family excited about it, too. I wish I could have been there to see them in action. I know I would have been very proud.

Anyway, Jessi arrived at the Pikes' house at ten o'clock on the nose and rang the bell. After several minutes, she heard a thundering of footsteps on the stairs. The door flew open and Mallory shouted, "Vanessa and Nicky are in the dining room. Watch them, will you?"

Then she disappeared from sight.

"Mal?" Jessi called, stepping into the foyer. "Where are you?"

"I'm being held captive by the Green Patrol," a muffled voice yelled from the living room.

Jessi stuck her head around a corner and found the triplets, Adam, Byron, and Jordan pinning Mallory's hands behind her back. Each boy wore a green baseball cap, with the bill turned backwards.

"The Green Patrol. What's that?" Jessi asked.

Jordan put his hands on his hips and stood with his feet apart. "We're here to guard against household waste."

Byron pointed to Mallory. "She was caught drinking water out of a paper cup."

Mal looked at me and shrugged. "At least it wasn't Styrofoam."

"But why use paper that you throw away when you can reuse a glass?" Adam demanded.

"She was also caught using paper towels in the kitchen," Jordan added. "She should have dried her hands on a cloth towel."

Mal rolled her eyes at Jessi, then turned back to her brothers. "I promise I'll never do it again."

"You better not," Byron warned. "But just to make sure, you have to go to Green school."

"No, not Green school!" Mal groaned. "Not again."

"What's that?" Jessi whispered.

Mal gestured with her head to a blackboard that had been set up on the other side of the living room. Standing in front of it was the youngest Pike, five-year-old Claire. Beside her stood Margo, the seven-year-old, her arms folded sternly across her chest.

"Bring Mallory here!" Claire ordered. "She has to read the rules."

Jessi followed Mal and the triplets over to the blackboard. "I didn't know everyone in your family was taking Dawn and Stacey's class."

"They're not," Mal murmured out of the side of her mouth. "But Vanessa and Nicky told them about it and they got so excited they formed the Green Patrol. They've been acting like this ever since last night."

"What do your parents think?" Jessi asked.

"They think it's cute," Mallory replied. "But they haven't been arrested by the Green Patrol yet, and forced to go to Green school. This is my third trip through."

"Okay, Mal," Margo commanded, "read the blackboard."

Mal sighed and began to read off each hand-printed line.

"I promise never to use plastic bags at the grocery store.

"I promise to use dishcloths instead of paper towels.

"I promise to carry my lunch in a lunch box, not a paper sack.

"I promise to recycle all cans and bottles whenever I can."

While Mallory spoke, Jessi checked on Vanessa and Nicky, who were sitting at the dining room table, hard at work on the Save the Planet assignments Dawn had given them. Each one wore the Kids Care badge.

"Help, Jessi!" Nicky called out the moment he saw her come into the room. "I don't know what to say in my letter."

"Who are you writing?" Jessi asked, peering over his shoulder. A yellow tablet was in front of him and a thick pencil was clutched in his hand.

Nicky raised his eyebrows and said, "The President."

"*The* President?" Jessi repeated. "You mean, of the United States?"

"Uh-huh."

"It's part of our assignment in Dawn and Stacey's class," Vanessa explained as she pulled an envelope out of an open box of pink stationery by her elbow. "We're supposed to write the world leaders and tell them how much we care about our planet." She pointed to several addressed envelopes piled neatly on the table. "I've already finished four letters."

"Do you mind if I read one?" Jessi asked.

"Here's my latest. It's supposed to go to Europe." Vanessa handed her the slip of pink paper. "Now I'm going to write Japan."

Jessi took the letter and read it aloud.

Dear Mrs. Queen of England,
My name is Vanessa Pike. I'm nine years old and I'm very upset about the pollution in the world. If we don't stop throwing garbage in our oceans, and polluting our air, animals and fish could die. Things are getting so bad that I'm afraid the world won't

be a very nice place when I grow up and have chil-
dren. Please help stop pollution.

> *Sincerely,*
> *Vanessa Pike*

Jessi looked up from the letter and smiled warmly at Vanessa. "That's really wonderful. I think the Queen will be impressed."

Nicky, who had been chewing anxiously on his pencil eraser asked, "Can I copy it?"

Vanessa shook her head. "No, Nicky. We're each supposed to write our own."

Jessi handed Vanessa's letter back to her and said, "Nicky, let me see what you've written."

"It's terrible," Nicky cried, covering the page with his arm.

"I'm sure it's not," Jessi prodded gently. "Let me see."

Slowly Nicky pulled his arm away. The page was blank except for three words written across the top: *Dear Mr. President.*

Jessi stared at them and said, "Well that's a good start. Now you just need to write the letter."

"I can't." Nicky's lower lip was trembling dangerously. "I know what I want to say, but I don't know how to spell all the words."

Jessi's sister Becca is the same age as Nicky, so Jessi is pretty good at handling eight-year-olds. "I've got an idea. How about if I act as your secretary?" she suggested. "You tell me what you want to say and I'll write it down."

Vanessa, who was busily writing her letter to Japan, lifted her head to protest, "But it has to be in Nicky's handwriting."

"Then Nicky can copy what I've written," Jessi replied as she sat down beside Mal's brother. She picked up the pencil and said, "All right, you've got 'Dear Mr. President.' Now what?"

Nicky scratched his chin and wandered around the table muttering to himself. Here's the letter he finally dictated to Jessi:

Dear Mr. President,

You don't know me but I've seen you on TV. My name is Nicky Pike and I'm in second grade at Stoneybrook Elementary School. I have a pet hamster named Frodo and seven brothers and sisters. Garbage is taking over the world and if we're not careful, there won't be any room left for my family or Frodo. Plus the air is bad for us. So, will you do me a favor and help fix this? Thank you.

Your friend,
Nicholas Pike

P.S. I'm sending my picture so you will know me the next time you see me.

Jessi helped Nicky copy the letter and address the envelope. But before they could start another letter, the Green Patrol burst into the dining room. The triplets circled the table, joined by Margo and Claire.

"Is that recycled paper?" Adam asked, pointing to the stationery they'd used.

Jessi examined Nicky's yellow tablet and nodded. "Yes, I think so."

"How about *that*?" Jordan pointed to the box of pink stationery and Vanessa's eyes widened in horror.

Margo folded her arms across her chest. "*You're* the one who told us we had to use recycled paper."

"I know I did," Vanessa muttered as she checked the outside of the box. "But I didn't buy this. Mom and Dad gave it to me for Christmas last year."

Mallory stepped into the room. "I think maybe the Green Patrol shouldn't worry about the stuff we already have. You guys should just focus on the future. So from now on, Vanessa will make sure she buys only recycled stationery. Right, Vanessa?"

Vanessa shot Mallory a grateful smile. "Right."

Mallory clapped her hands together. "Now, I think it's time we had some lunch. Mom made PBJs for everybody before she left this morning."

"Hooray!" Claire cried. "I love peanut butter."

Jessi helped stack the letters in a neat pile on the sideboard, and then she and Mal led the group into the kitchen.

"Uh-oh," Nicky shouted as they entered the big family kitchen. "Water leak!" He pointed to the dripping kitchen faucet.

Adam leapt forward. "Who should the Green Patrol arrest?"

Mal rolled her eyes at Jessi. "I don't think you need to arrest anybody," she told Adam in her most patient voice. "I think you just need to make sure the faucet is completely turned off."

"I'll do it," Margo called, racing for the sink.

"Maybe we should check all the faucets in the house," Vanessa suggested. "Dawn told us that even the tiniest leaky faucet can lose up to three thousand gallons of water a year."

"How much is that?" Claire wondered.

"She said that's like drinking sixty-five glasses of water a day for a whole year."

"Wow!"

The kids stared at the kitchen sink and tried to imagine drinking that much water.

"We better check out the rest of the house right away," Adam declared with a worried frown. "We've got lots of faucets and showers."

Jessi grabbed his arm before he could leave the kitchen. "Lunch first. Then we can check the house, plus the spigots outside."

"Outside?" Jordan repeated.

"Sure," Jessi said. "Garden hoses can leak, too, you know."

The prospect of inspecting not just the house but outside, too, cheered everyone.

Mal's mother had set the sandwiches on a big plate on the counter. Next to them was a plastic baggie filled with celery and carrot sticks.

"Uh-oh." Nicky pointed to the baggie. "The Green Patrol may have to arrest Mom. She used plastic."

"Not so fast," Mal said. "It's not a waste. We can use this bag again. I'll rinse it out and then put it in the dish drainer to dry. How does that sound?"

Nicky and Vanessa exchanged looks, and then Vanessa said, "I guess that's okay."

"What a relief," Jessi murmured under her breath. Picking up a roll of paper towels, she said, "Okay, everybody, take your sandwiches to the table."

"Look out!" Jordan shouted. "Jessi's going to waste paper. Green patrol!"

Jessi pulled her hand back quickly. "If we can't put our sandwiches on paper towels," she asked Mallory, "what should we do about cleaning up crumbs, and wiping our mouths?"

"I know!" Margo cried, "Let's use *real* plates and cloth napkins."

Mallory smiled. "That's using your head."

While the kids put their sandwiches on glass saucers, Jessi muttered under her breath, "Is it all right to give the kids glasses of milk to drink?"

"Sure," Mallory replied. "Why wouldn't it be?"

"I don't know," she said with a shrug. "Maybe milking cows is bad for the animals."

Mallory laughed. "The Green Patrol has really shaken you up, hasn't it?"

Jessi nodded her head. "I'm afraid to breathe. I might pollute the air."

After the kids ate lunch, they made a complete inspection of the house and yard. Several times Jessi and Mal made mistakes. Jessi found a soda can by the fence and threw it in the trash. She forgot to recycle. And Mallory left the light on in the kitchen. She was wasting energy. But the Green Patrol was right there to tell them about it.

By the time Mr. and Mrs. Pike arrived home two hours later, the house and yard had been given a complete Green Inspection, and Jessi and Mal were totally exhausted.

They had both been forced to attend Green school five times and, according to Jessi, "Once was more than enough!"

CHAPTER 8

I spent most of the week planning a recycling program for Stoneybrook Middle School. First I designed a poster listing reasons why SMS was the ideal site for a recycling center. Then I drew up a schedule for taking the cans and bottles to the main terminal downtown. I'd even made a chart of how many students would be needed to work on the project each week, and how many hours they would have to spend a month to keep the recycling center going.

On Thursday I got up my courage to present my plan to Mrs. Gonzalez. After school, I went to her classroom and told her about it. Her response was better than I ever expected.

"Dawn, that's an excellent idea," she said. "I'm really impressed."

"Thanks," I said proudly. "When can we start? Tomorrow?"

Mrs. Gonzalez laughed. "Not so fast. These things take time."

"But there isn't any time," I protested. "Every day the world gets covered with more and more garbage. You said so yourself."

Mrs. Gonzalez folded her hands in front of her on her desk. "I'm glad to see you're so enthusiastic about this, and I have a feeling you could really make it work. But before we can start anything, Mr. Kingbridge will have to okay it."

My stomach did a flip-flop. Mr. Kingbridge was the vice-principal and a visit to his office was always pretty scary.

"I'll talk to him this afternoon." Mrs. Gonzalez slid her chair back and stood up. "We'll see if you can show him your presentation tomorrow."

"Great." I swallowed hard.

At home that night I practiced a speech over and over in front of the mirror. Then I performed it for Mary Anne and her kitten Tigger. At breakfast the next morning, I presented it to my mom and Richard. By the time I talked to Mr. Kingbridge that afternoon, I had memorized it completely.

Mr. Kingbridge was sitting behind his big oak desk when Mrs. Downey, the school secretary, ushered me into his office. He gestured for me to sit down, then said, "Your teacher,

Mrs. Gonzalez, is very impressed with you. She says you have an idea that will benefit not just our school but the whole town of Stoneybrook. Is that right?"

I swallowed hard and croaked, "Yes, sir."

"Well." Mr. Kingbridge leaned back in his chair and clasped his hands behind his head. "Tell me about it."

I decided to stand up to make my speech, because that's how I had been practicing it. I was a little shaky at first (A little? My hands were quivering!) but after I showed him my poster and listed the reasons why SMS should be a recycling center, I started to calm down.

"SMS is in a prime location for a recycling center — it's only a few minutes walk from lots of neighborhoods," I explained. "Having this center on our school grounds would train the students to be ecology-minded and they in turn would train their families."

Mr. Kingbridge nodded his head and leaned forward as I continued my presentation. After I showed him the work schedule, and the plans for transporting the cans and bottles to the main center, I announced in a clear, strong voice, "Mr. Kingbridge, this project will not only benefit the community by giving them a convenient location to recycle but it will also benefit our school. Just think of the hundreds of pieces of paper we use here everyday that could easily be recycled. I bet our school cafeteria provides over a thousand cartons of milk a week to the students."

"That's a lot of paper," Mr. Kingbridge agreed.

"And the teachers' lounge has a soft drink machine. Those cans should be recycled. Why not let the students of SMS do something good for our school and our planet?"

When I'd finished Mr. Kingbridge asked to look at my notebook once more. After studying it for a few minutes, he raised his head. "How much is this going to cost?"

"It won't cost anyone a thing, but time."

"What about the supplies?"

"All we need are clearly labeled cardboard boxes that we can get free from grocery stores, and a dry place to store them."

"How about advertising?"

"We can make posters at my house and put them up around town."

"We?" Mr. Kingbridge arched his eyebrows. "Who's we?"

"The students at SMS."

Mr. Kingbridge stared at me for a moment. Then he got up from his desk and looked out his window, his hands behind his back. After what seemed like a million years, he said, "If you can prove to me that the students at SMS support you, and are willing to work very hard to make this project succeed . . ." (he paused and then smiled) "then I see no reason why you can't start your recycling program."

"All right!"

I shouted so loudly that the sound surprised even me, and I clapped my hand over my mouth.

Mr. Kingbridge didn't seem to mind. In fact, little smile lines formed around his eyes as he said, "This really is a worthwhile project, Dawn. I'll give you a week and a half to drum up interest and then we'll discuss it again. Good luck. I hope it works."

I was smiling so hard when I left Mr. Kingbridge's office that my cheeks ached. All I had to do to get his okay was prove that the students at SMS were interested. That would be easy!

That night I began my campaign. First I called everyone in the BSC and asked them to help me make posters and talk to the students. The next morning Mary Anne and I went to school early because I wanted to greet the students as they came in through the front doors.

Mary Anne agreed to help hold my sign, which read: "SMS needs a Recycling Center. *You* can make it happen!"

The first person to come by was Erica Blumberg from our homeroom. She was juggling her books and what looked like her breakfast — a small can of orange juice and half a piece of buttered toast. I caught her math book just before it hit the floor and tucked it back into her book bag.

"Thanks," she mumbled as she finished off the last bite of her toast.

"Erica, I need your help," I began. "I'm trying to start a recycling center here at school."

"What can I do?"

"Pass the word to all your friends, and volunteer to be a helper when the project gets going."

"Sure," Erica said as she took a final swig of her juice. "Just keep me posted."

She was about to toss the empty container in the trash can by the front door when I shouted, "Erica! Are you crazy?"

Erica leaped back from the trash can as if a deadly snake were inside it. Her book bag slipped off her shoulder and clattered onto the floor. "What? What's the matter?"

I pointed to the can in her hand. "That's an aluminum can. Never throw it away. It can be recycled."

"Oh. Sorry." Erica turned in a confused circle, trying to figure out what to do with her can.

"Look, I'll take that for you," Mary Anne offered as she picked up Erica's book bag.

"And when the school gets its own center, you can just drop it in the box."

"Oh, thanks, Mary Anne," Erica said gratefully. She hurried down the hall and didn't even look at me when she said, "I guess I'll see you later."

Mary Anne turned to me and hissed, "Why did you shout at Erica like that?"

"She was going to throw that can away," I shot back. "Do you know how bad that is for the environment?"

"Yes," Mary Anne replied with an impatient sigh. "You've already told me a hundred times."

"Well, then you should have stopped her, too. Americans throw away sixty-five billion cans a year. Do you know how much garbage that is?" I hate to admit it but I was starting to get upset with Mary Anne. She didn't seem to care as much as I did about what we were trying to do. "I thought you believed in recycling."

"I do, but I'm not going to yell at everyone just because they throw away one can or bottle," Mary Anne said. "And you'd better be careful how you treat people, or they will turn against you and your idea. Here."

She shoved my poster into my hands and started to walk away.

"Hey, where are you going?" I asked.

"I've got to get to class early to finish some homework," Mary Anne said without looking back.

Now I was really confused. Mary Anne seemed upset with me, but she had no right to be. I was just doing my part to help save the environment.

After Mary Anne left, I talked to about twenty more kids before the bell rang. Then I hurried down the hall to my locker, where I ran into Shawna Riverson. Her locker is next to mine, and it's a pigsty (which is a big surprise, since she is always so perfect-looking). Anyway, when Shawna opened her locker, I swear, three plastic cups, some greasy wrappers from month-old hamburgers, and two yellow Styrofoam containers tumbled onto the hall floor. (Gag!)

"You must live on burgers and fries," I said as I watched her scoop up the debris.

"Who can eat the food they serve here?" Shawna groaned. "They practically force me to go to Burger Town."

I watched as she shoved the Styrofoam containers, along with the rest of her trash, back in her locker. "Well next time you get a hamburger, tell them to just put it in a paper bag," I told her. "Styrofoam is terrible for the environment."

"I'm sure," she said sarcastically, "that two boxes are not going to hurt anybody."

I don't know what came over me but suddenly I got really angry. "That's permanent garbage. Don't you understand? It'll never go away. Those two containers will probably float around in the ocean and kill innocent sea turtles."

"Big deal."

Shawna shut her locker door and began walking down the hall. I followed her all the way to homeroom, trying to make her come to her senses. "It is a *very* big deal. Do you know that the chemicals used to make Styrofoam are ruining the ozone layer?" (I didn't realize it but I was practically shouting.) "That causes the greenhouse effect, which is why the Northeast is having a drought right now, and why Texas is getting waterlogged."

"So tell them to get an umbrella," Shawna said as we stepped into our homeroom.

Several of the students in class laughed at her reply, which just made me even more angry. How could they laugh about something as important as the future of our world? I would have said something really nasty if the bell hadn't rung.

Mary Anne, who sits behind me in homeroom, tugged on my arm. "Calm down,

Dawn," she whispered. "Class is about to start."

I slumped down in my seat, feeling more convinced than ever that what I was doing was right.

CHAPTER 9

Boy, Jessi and Mal, you wernt kidding when you said that all the kids have cauht the Green bug. From the moment I arrived at the Johansens, Charlot chatered non-stop about saving the plant. Then I walked her over to Stacy's for her class and boy, was i impressed! Dawn and Stacey — you guys are rilly terrific teachers. Even I lerned something!

Claudia arrived at our Save the Planet class on Thursday completely out of breath. She told us that Charlotte had insisted on running the entire way. This was a very important day for our class because we were making our final preparations for the Green Fair and Charlotte wanted to make sure she didn't miss a thing.

The minute they walked in the door, I took charge.

"Coats on the hooks in the hall," I instructed. "Guests on the couch. And students check the assignment sheet posted by the kitchen door." I clapped my hands together several times. "We've got a lot of things to do today so let's not dawdle."

Stacey, who had been in the kitchen when Claudia first arrived, was a lot more casual. "Hi, Claud!" she called. "Can I get you something to drink? Juice or mineral water?"

Claud shook her head. "Don't worry about me. I'm going to be as quiet as a mouse, and just sit over here in the corner."

Stacey was carrying some sheets of poster board and a pack of colored markers in her hands as she stepped into the living room. "Did you see what Woody Jefferson and Trevor Sandbourne brought for lunch today?" she asked.

Claudia had eaten with some friends on the

other side of the lunch room. She leaned forward eagerly. "No. What?"

"Brie cheese, *paté*, and a bottle of sparkling cider."

"You're kidding!" Claudia gasped. "I can't believe I missed this."

"They even spread out a red-and-white checkered tablecloth, and brought their own silver and a couple of wine glasses. Mrs. Ensign thought they were drinking real wine and nearly had a cow." (Mrs. Ensign is a lunchroom monitor.)

"Why'd they do it?" Claud asked.

"To prove that we don't have to eat Mystery Meat and pickled green beans to have a good lunch."

"Oooh, I bet that made Mrs. Ensign furious."

"Yeah," Stacey giggled, "you should have seen her. Her face turned beet-red. Trevor said he thought he saw steam coming out of her ears."

"*Excuse me?*" I cut in on their conversation. "I don't want to interrupt your gossip session, Stacey, but we *do* have a class to teach."

"Oops!" Stacey winced. "I'll talk to you later, Claud." She hurried over to the kids who were clustered around the assignment sheet chattering excitedly.

"I'm with Charlotte at the shopping bag

booth," Becca Ramsey said to Stacey. "What's that?"

Stacey opened her mouth to reply but I answered for her (after all, the booth was my idea). "We want to encourage people not to use paper or plastic when they buy their groceries," I explained. "We want them to bring their own bags. You two will be selling canvas shopping bags that you have decorated. You'll also sell plain ones that people can decorate on their own."

"That sounds fun," Charlotte said.

"I want to be at the shopping bag booth, too," Melody Korman added, pouting.

Stacey knelt beside her and said, "All of the booths are fun. I've talked to Bloomer's, the nursery on Spring Street, and they've agreed to donate small plants for the booth we would like you and Hannie to run."

"What do we do with the plants?" Melody asked.

"You sell them," I explained. "This is a very important booth. Not only does it raise money but it helps keep the world green."

A big smile lit up Melody's face and turning to Hannie she exclaimed, "Our booth will be the best one at the whole fair!"

"In the whole world!" Hannie replied.

Stacey handed Melody some poster board.

"Your assignment today is to make the sign for your booth."

Melody hurried over to a corner of the room, calling, "I'll make the letters, Hannie, if you'll draw a picture of a plant."

Hannie turned to Stacey. "Do you have a green magic marker?"

Stacey found one while I explained the rest of the assignments.

"The school has loaned us their button-making machine so Karen, Andrew, and Suzi will make *Think Green* and *My Kids Care* buttons, and sell them to the parents in the neighborhood."

"Yea!" Andrew and Suzi cheered.

"Bill and Buddy will be in charge of the wild animal booth."

"What's that?" Bill asked.

"You're going to show people how to save the animals. I want you guys to cut out pictures from magazines and make a collage of endangered species."

Bill and Buddy whispered to each other for a few moments. Finally Buddy declared, "We like that booth. But we would also like to sell something because I'm a good salesman."

Stacey and I had to think fast on that one. "What about those birdhouses?" she suggested.

The week before, the kids had made birdhouses out of milk cartons and decorated them.

"Great idea!" I said.

"My mom really liked the one I brought home," Bill said.

"We'll make millions of birdhouses," Buddy cried, hopping around the room in excitement, "and millions of dollars!"

"Ten birdhouses would probably be enough," I said, trying to keep a straight face. "But you two make as many as you can."

Stacey checked the list to see what was left. "We also have several demonstration booths," she said. "That's where we'll show the results of our experiments."

"You mean, we're going to let people look at our buried treasures that we dug up last week?" Karen Brewer wrinkled her nose. "Some of that stuff is rotten."

"It's supposed to be," I explained. "You see, the lettuce leaves and the apple core are decaying and becoming part of the earth."

"Does anybody remember what had happened to the Styrofoam and plastic wrap when we dug them up?" Stacey asked.

"I do," David Michael replied. "Nothing. They just got dirty."

"That's right," I said. "Because they aren't biodegradable. Which means that Styrofoam and plastic are really bad for our earth."

"I think Linny and David Michael should work this booth," Stacey said. "One of you could explain our projects to the visitors, while the other one points out the results of our experiments."

The two boys gave each other a high five, then proceeded to argue about who would do the talking and who would do the pointing.

"Next we'll have a letter writing booth," I said, smiling at the Pike kids. "I'm putting Nicky and Vanessa in charge of that one, since the letters they wrote to our world leaders were so good."

Nicky stuck out his lower lip. "If my letter was so good, how come the President hasn't written me back? I check the mailbox every day."

Stacey took Nicky's hand. "The President is a very busy man. He barely has time to read his letters, let alone answer them. But I'm sure he liked yours, especially since you sent him your picture."

"You really think so?" Nicky asked.

"I'm sure of it." Stacey gave him a quick hug and then stood up. "All right. Everyone break into groups, and start working on your projects. When you're — "

"Not so fast," I said, cutting Stacey off. "First I want to know how many of you called your friends to find out if their families recycle?"

Only two kids raised their hands — Bill and Melody Korman. I shook my head. "I'm really disappointed in the rest of you. How can we save the planet if you can't even make one phone call?"

The kids who only moments before had big smiles on their faces, hung their heads and stared at the carpet.

"Now next week, when I ask this question," I said, "I want every single one of you to raise your hand. Will you do that?" I waited till they nodded, then said, "Good. Now let's get to work."

When the class was over, and the kids were getting ready to go home, Claudia approached Stacey and me.

"You guys are incredible," she said. "You look like real pros. No wonder Charlotte is so excited about this class. If there's anything I can do to help your fair, just let me know."

"Well . . . there is *one* thing," I said.

"Name it," Claudia said.

"Would you mind designing some fliers that we can hand out at school? We'd love to have your artistic touch."

Stacey looked at me in surprise. "But I thought we were going to ask the kids to do that."

I rolled my eyes and whispered, "We *were*. But if we can get a real artist like Claudia to do them, they'll look professional and more people will come."

Stacey gave me a funny look, then shrugged. "Okay. If that's what you want."

"It's what we both want. Isn't it?"

"I guess so." She sighed.

I couldn't believe her response. Stacey hardly sounded interested in the project at all.

"You guys?" Claudia looked a little embarrassed to have overheard us. "Look, I don't want to interfere. Maybe it would be better if the kids made the fliers."

"No!" I practically shouted. "I want you to do the work. They'll look better."

Claudia glanced from me to Stacey and said, "Okay. Would you mind if I asked Charlotte to help me?"

That made Stacey smile. "I think that's a wonderful idea, Claudia."

Charlotte liked the idea a lot, too. On the walk back to her house, she chattered about it nonstop.

"I'm so glad you're going to help us save the world, Claudia," she said. "We really need you."

Claudia was still feeling inspired from the class. She wrapped her arm around Charlotte's shoulder and hugged her. "I'm glad I can help. This is a wonderful project."

The two of them spent the rest of the afternoon working on designs for the flier. Charlotte thought they should start with a picture of the earth in the center. Then Claudia suggested they draw a line of kids holding hands that ringed the globe. They agreed to cut the shapes of the earth and children out of construction paper, then glue them onto a white background.

"We can cut the letters out of ads in magazines," Claudia suggested after they'd finished with the construction paper. "That will make the flier look like a crazy quilt."

"Oooh!" Charlotte clapped her hands together excitedly. "That would be really cool."

By the time Dr. Johanssen arrived home, Claudia and Charlotte were finished. They proudly displayed their design to Charlotte's mother, who said, "This class has been the best thing to happen to Charlotte in a long time. I can't remember when she's been so excited about something."

Claudia nodded so hard her earrings (which were made of paper clips and sequins and ribbon) bounced. "It's even gotten me excited," she said. "Dawn and Stacey have really done a great job."

That night Claud intended to call Stacey and

me to congratulate us, but Stacey called her first.

"Dawn is driving me crazy!" Stacey complained the second Claud answered.

"What are you talking about?" Claudia said as she propped up her bed pillows and leaned back against them. She fumbled behind the headboard for the bag of Mallomars she'd stashed there. She had a feeling this was going to be a long call (and she was right).

"You saw how she acted today," Stacey said. "Didn't you notice anything unusual?"

"Well, she did seem a little bossy at times."

"A *little*!" Stacey shouted into the phone. "She barely let me finish a sentence."

"Well, maybe that's her way of showing how excited she is about the project," Claud said diplomatically.

"It's her way of showing everyone that she's right and I'm wrong. She acts as if she was the first person to discover pollution."

"Whoa," Claud said, taking a bite of her Mallomar, "I didn't realize you were so upset."

"It's been building up for the past few weeks," Stacey admitted. "In the beginning, we divided up what we had to do but now she insists on being in charge of everything."

"Have you talked to her about it?"

"I've tried," Stacey said. "But every time I start to say something, she changes the subject by pointing out some mistake I've made, like using a paper napkin instead of a cloth one."

Claud tore open a second Mallomar. "We all agree that Dawn has gone kind of overboard about ecology, but you shouldn't let it get to you. I mean, how bad can it be?"

"Well, to tell you the truth," Stacey said in a sad voice, "if I didn't feel so committed to the kids in our class, I would probably just quit and do another project for Mrs. Gonzalez."

Claudia gulped down a big bite. "It's that serious?"

"It's that serious," Stacey confided. "And I'm afraid that if something doesn't change soon, it's going to ruin my friendship with Dawn. Permanently."

CHAPTER 10

"May I have your attention, please? This is Dawn Schafer. Today I want to talk to you about a very important subject — recycling."

Mr. Kingbridge had let me make a speech over the school's PA system during homeroom announcements. I felt weird talking into a microphone, and knowing that every kid in school was listening. I might have felt nervous, too, but I had written my speech down, so all I had to do was read it.

I told everyone about the need for a recycling center, and why SMS was the perfect location. Then I finished with a challenge.

"I want every student at SMS to stand up and show you care. How can you do that? By casting your vote for a recycling center and volunteering to help run it. Because, if you don't care about our planet — who will?"

Questionnaires were to be handed out after my speech to every student in each homeroom. Mr. Kingbridge had drawn them up himself. Then he got on the microphone and told everyone how to fill them out. "Don't sign your names," he added. "This is a general survey to find out your interest and willingness to participate in the recycling program designed by Dawn Schafer."

The last question in the survey asked the students to name an appropriate chairperson for the recycling project. My name was listed first. Then came Mrs. Gonzalez's name, and finally a blank space marked, *Other, please specify.*

The questionnaires were collected by the teachers and turned into the office. I was a nervous wreck waiting for the results. I talked to Kristy and Mary Anne about it at lunchtime.

"It's taking an awfully long time for them to figure out the results," I worried.

"Are you afraid they won't pick you as chairperson?" Kristy asked, sliding her tray onto the table next to mine.

"No, of course not," I replied. "It's my idea. Why wouldn't they pick me? I'm afraid they'll vote against the project."

"I'm sure everyone'll go for it," Mary Anne said. "It's a great idea. Why wouldn't they want to do it?"

I opened my milk carton and took a long

sip. "I'm worried that half the students don't know what recycling is."

"Oh, they know about it," Claudia said, laughing, as she joined us at the table. "Every square inch of this school is covered with posters."

"That's right," Kristy said. "And every student got your newsletter in homeroom."

Mary Anne dipped her spoon into her bowl of tomato soup. "And I know for a fact that you have given your speech to every student who has walked through the front doors of this school."

"That must be why everyone is using the back entrance," Claudia joked. "They're afraid they'll hear Dawn's lecture again."

"If they don't know about recycling, they'd have to be deaf and blind," Kristy concluded.

I nibbled on a carrot stick. "I hope you're right. I'm just worried that nobody cares enough to make it happen. Let's face it, most of the kids here are pretty apathetic."

"Well, you've done your part." Mary Anne patted my arm. "You've told them about your program. You can't *make* people care. That's up to them."

"I know, I know." I held up my crossed fingers. "Let's just hope they do."

Stacey hadn't said anything during our

lunch conversation, which was a little weird. But she'd been that way a lot lately. I figured she had other worries on her mind. Like her big test in history. But just as lunch ended, she said, "They'll vote for the recycling center so don't think about it." I was about to say thanks, when she added, "There are much bigger problems you should be worrying about."

Before I could ask Stacey what she meant, the bell rang and she hurried out of the lunch room.

Mr. Kingbridge stopped me in the hall on the way to my next class. "Dawn, the office staff is tallying the votes. We should have the results by the end of the day."

"Thanks, Mr. Kingbridge," I said, after the butterflies in my stomach calmed down. "I hope it's good news."

"Me, too," he said, patting me on the shoulder. "Me, too."

I could barely concentrate in my next classes. All I could think about was the hard work I'd already put into the recycling program. I'd made phone calls, tacked up posters, typed up the newsletter — I'd even written notes to all of the club presidents and made a speech at a student council meeting. Mary Anne was right. There was really nothing more I could do.

During the last hour of the day I sat at my desk with my hands clasped tightly in front of me. My heart was beating so loudly I barely heard a word my teacher was saying. Then, five minutes before the end of class, Mr. Kingbridge's voice came crackling over the loudspeaker.

"May I have your attention, please? Your attention, please."

Everyone stopped what they were doing and listened attentively.

"I am very pleased to announce the results of this morning's questionnaire."

My heart started pounding a mile a minute. This sounded like good news but I didn't want to jump to any conclusions.

"By an overwhelming majority, the students of Stoneybrook Middle School have indicated that they would like to host Stoneybrook's new recycling center."

Cheers rang out from the students around the room but no one was cheering louder than me. In fact, I was shouting so loudly I barely heard the rest of the announcement.

"And as their leader for this project, the students have selected . . . Mrs. Estelle Gonzalez."

The smile on my face froze. I blinked several times. Had I heard correctly?

"So all those interested in helping to start

Stoneybrook Middle School's recycling program," Mr. Kingbridge continued, "please sign up with Mrs. Gonzalez."

I *had* heard correctly. The students had voted for Mrs. Gonzalez, not me.

The cheering tapered off into excited talking. Amelia Freeman, who sat in front of me, turned around and gave me a sympathetic look. I tried to act nonchalant.

"I'm sure the students chose Mrs. Gonzalez because they wanted someone older to head this important project," I said to her. "Of course, Mrs. Gonzalez will use me as the student representative."

"I'm sure you're right," Amelia said with an encouraging smile.

The more I thought about it, the more it made sense to me. Of course the students would want Mrs. Gonzalez to head the recycling center. After all, she was an adult, and that might make lots of things easier for us. Recycling companies and city officials would probably feel better dealing with a teacher than with a student.

By the time I reached my locker after school, I had almost recovered from the blow of not being elected. Then I made the mistake of getting a drink from the water fountain. Two girls, whose voices I recognized as those of Cokie Mason and Grace Blume, were talking just around the corner and I overheard every word they said.

"I'm glad the recycling program is going to happen here," Grace said. "I voted for it. Did you?"

"Yeah," Cokie answered. "But I *didn't* vote for Dawn Schafer to run it."

"Me, neither. She's been so obnoxious, acting like none of us have any brains."

"No kidding. I heard Mrs. Gonzalez won by a landslide."

"Yeah, she did."

Cokie giggled and added, "I bet the only people in this whole school who voted for Dawn are her friends in that baby-sitting club."

I couldn't believe my ears. People thought I was obnoxious! And not just a few, either. It sounded as if the whole school hated me.

I had never felt so humiliated in my entire life. All I wanted to do was hide. I waited until Cokie and Grace had gone, and then I raced into the girls' bathroom. I couldn't bear the thought of facing anyone. I intended to wait there until all the kids at school had gone home.

When I reached the bathroom I looked at myself in the mirror and burst into tears. They poured down my cheeks but I didn't even try to stop them. Now I knew what Stacey had meant when she told me I had bigger things to worry about. First I felt hurt, then I felt ashamed, then I felt angry that my fellow students could've done this to me. All I had wanted was to do something good. And this was the thanks I got.

I stood in the bathroom for at least half an hour crying. By the time I left, my eyes were puffy and red, but I was too miserable to care.

CHAPTER 11

"Dawn, hurry!" Mary Anne shouted from downstairs. "We're going to be late for the opening ceremonies."

It was Saturday, the official opening day for the Stoneybrook Middle School Recycling Center. The band was going to play while Mrs. Gonzalez cut the big red ribbon that had been strung across the row of recycling bins in the parking lot. Then the mayor of Stoneybrook would give a speech.

"I'm coming," I shouted as I ran a brush through my hair one last time.

I had been standing in front of the mirror for forty-five minutes, trying to fix my hair. I'd pulled it into a ponytail on the side, then a French braid down the center of my back, but nothing looked right. Finally I just let it fall straight past my shoulders. I don't know why I was worrying so much about my appearance. I wasn't even going to be involved in the ceremony.

That was partly my fault, I guess. Once the project had been taken away from me, I hadn't felt like doing anything to help create the recycling center. In fact, for a while I thought if I even heard the word recycle again, I'd scream.

Mrs. Gonzalez did ask me to be in charge of the newsletter and I couldn't very well have said no. I mean, she *was* my teacher, and pretty soon she'd be grading my science project.

"The newsletter is the most important part of this project," she had told me. "It will go to all of the parents of students at SMS, and be distributed to the library, banks, and the grocery stores and merchants downtown. I know you can make it a good one."

She didn't add that it was one project that didn't require me to work with anyone else. But I got the picture.

I worked really hard on the newsletter, anyway. I wanted to show Cokie and Grace and all the students at SMS that they couldn't defeat me. But I didn't volunteer to do anything else for the center. I didn't paint signs or distribute fliers. I didn't even offer to help out on opening day. And nobody asked me to. I guess that was what was bugging me.

"Dawn?" Mary Anne stuck her head into my room. "Are you okay?"

"Sure." I turned around to face her and plastered a smile on my face. I held up my brush. "I was just trying to comb a few knots out of my hair."

"Oh." Mary Anne came into the room and sat on the edge of my bed, watching me carefully. "I thought you might be feeling a little, um, weird about today."

Leave it to Mary Anne to know what I was thinking.

"I mean, this was your idea," she continued. "And they didn't even put your picture in the paper."

The *Stoneybrook News* had sent a reporter and a photographer to our school on Friday. They'd interviewed Mrs. Gonzalez and the vice-principal and asked a few of the students who were putting last minute touches on the recycling bins to pose for them. Mrs. Gonzalez had mentioned my name to the reporter but hadn't suggested they photograph me, too.

That hurt. I didn't want to admit it, though. Not even to Mary Anne. So I tried to laugh it off.

"My name was already in the article three times," I said. "I guess they figured a photo would go to my head."

Mary Anne gave my shoulders a squeeze.

"Well, if it means anything to you, I think your picture should have been in the paper. I also think you should be the one cutting the ribbon today."

I shrugged. "The students elected Mrs. Gonzalez to head the project. She really should do it."

"Dawn!"

This time it was my mother calling from the kitchen. "Do we have to separate the plastic bottles from the glass?"

"Yes!" I called as Mary Anne and I came down the stairs. "And it would help if you separated the clear glass from the brown and green."

My mother was standing in the center of the kitchen surrounded by paper bags and cardboard boxes. "This is a lot of work," she said, blowing a strand of hair off her forehead.

"Not really," I said, tossing a green bottle into a separate box. "Once you have the proper containers, recycling should only take about fifteen minutes of your time a week."

The kitchen door opened and Richard came inside. "Well, the trunk's full," he announced. "It looks like we'll have to put the rest of this stuff in the backseat."

"Oh, dear." My mother wrinkled her nose. "Won't that be messy?"

Richard (who is Mr. Neatnik) shook his head. "I've covered the seat with trash bags."

I patted my mother on the shoulder. "Don't worry, Mom, it will never be as big a load as this again. Now that the recycling center is open, we can make one trip a week."

Richard picked up two more boxes and paused as he passed me. "Dawn, you should be very proud of yourself. This recycling center is good for the entire town."

I smiled but didn't say anything. I hadn't told a soul about what I'd heard in the hall the day the election results were announced. I was too embarrassed.

In fact, my mom and Richard had no idea how hard it was going to be for me to watch the opening ceremonies.

"Now according to this newsletter," my mother said as the four of us headed for the car, "all we have to do is drive into the parking lot at SMS, and students will take care of the sorting. Is that right?"

"I think so," I said. "Then later on today, parent volunteers will move the bins over to the main recycling center downtown, and empty them."

"Somebody had to do a lot of planning to make this happen," Richard said.

"You can thank Dawn for that," Mary Anne

said, wrapping her arm around my shoulder. "She drew up the entire plan and gave it to Mrs. Gonzalez."

My mother checked her watch. "We'd better get a move on if we're going to make the opening ceremonies."

"There's no need to hurry," I said. "The band plays first, and you know how terrible they can be."

Mary Anne giggled. "They have to announce the name of the song before they play it. Otherwise no one would ever recognize the tune."

Our car was so packed with bottles and newspapers that the four of us had to cram into the front seat. I sat in Mary Anne's lap. We arrived at the school with two minutes to spare.

As we pulled into the parking lot, my stomach felt as if it were tied in knots. Colorful flags waved from poles bordering the recycling station, with a banner stretched between them. It looked like a carnival, or a county fair. The recycling bins had been painted in reds, yellows, blues, and greens. On either side of each bin stood a student volunteer, ready to help people sort their trash.

"Hey!" Mary Anne leaned forward and peered through the windshield. "There's Claudia and everyone!"

The members of the BSC were gathered around a health food stand that had been set up by the entrance to the parking lot. They were clutching large bran muffins, laughing and joking together as they ate.

"Dawn, do you want me to drop you off here?" Richard joked. "It looks like there are enough muffins at that table to last you a week."

I tried to laugh but only a weak chuckle came out. "No, thanks. I've already eaten." It wasn't that I didn't want to see my friends. It's just that I didn't feel much like socializing with anyone.

Mary Anne shot me a worried glance. She knew what I was going through. "We can catch up with them later," she whispered to me.

Richard backed the car up to the bins and got out to open the trunk. He was met by Pete Black, who said, "Here's a raffle ticket, sir. Thank you for recycling."

"A raffle ticket?" my mother's ears perked up. "What's the prize?"

"A dinner for two at Chez Maurice, plus two tickets to the movie of your choice at the Stoneybrook Cinema."

"Sounds great," Richard replied.

Then Emily Bernstein stepped forward. "Here's a pamphlet explaining why recycling is so good for the earth and a form to fill out if you want to subscribe to *P3*."

"*P3*?" Mary Anne tossed a box of colored glass in the red bin. "What's that?"

I answered before Emily could. "*P3* is a terrific environmental magazine for kids."

"What does the 'P3' stand for?" Mary Anne asked.

Emily started to reply, then shrugged. "You know, I'm not really sure."

"Planet-3," I answered. "Which is Earth, the third planet from the sun."

Richard looped one arm across my shoulders and beamed proudly at me. "Hey, you really know your stuff!"

I should have felt wonderful but I didn't. I watched the student teams from SMS working together, smoothly directing parents to the different bins and handing out pamphlets. I felt like a total outsider.

This had been my idea. I was the one who had talked the vice-principal and the school into having a recycling center. Now I wasn't even a part of it.

"May I have your attention, please!" Mr. Kingbridge's voice came over the loudspeaker system that had been set up in the parking lot. "I'd like to welcome you to Stoneybrook Middle School's brand new recycling center."

Mr. Kingbridge looked strange. Usually he wore a black or gray suit, a white shirt, and some dull tie. Today he was dressed in a striped rugby shirt, jeans, and tennis shoes (but he still looked like a man who should have been in a suit).

"We are thrilled with the turnout today," Mr. Kingbridge continued. "Everyone, give yourselves a big hand!" He paused and squinted out at the crowd as we applauded. "The mayor of Stoneybrook is here because she believes what we are doing is very important to our school, to our community, and to the world. Isn't that right, Mayor Keane?"

The woman in the brown suit standing next to Mr. Kingbridge nodded pleasantly.

"And now, as we cut the ribbon, I'd like to introduce the person responsible for this project. If it hadn't been for her, today would never have happened."

That had to be me! I was going to be introduced after all. Mary Anne turned and smiled in my direction and my heart started beating faster as I waited for Mr. Kingbridge to announce my name.

"Ladies and gentlemen, let's give a big round of applause for Estelle Gonzalez."

The smile slid off of Mary Anne's face and she blurted out, "But what about Dawn?"

Luckily the clapping was so loud that nobody but me heard her. Otherwise I would have died of embarrassment.

The rest of the ceremony seemed to last for hours, though I know it was only a few minutes. At the end of the ribbon cutting the band played "America the Beautiful." Then the crowd broke up.

I couldn't wait to get back to the car. Mary Anne, after saying a quick hello to Kristy and the rest of the BSC, joined me in the backseat. "You should feel very proud of what you've done," she said as our parents got into the car.

"Maybe I should," I mumbled, folding my arms across my chest and slumping down in the seat. "But I don't. So let's just get out of here, okay?"

Neither of us said another word the entire trip home.

CHAPTER 12

Tuesday

Baby-sitting for the Kormans was for the birds! Seriously, we spent the entire afternoon building tree feeders and bird-houses. I think if Bill and Melody had yarn and needles we would have knitted little bird jackets. Dawn, you would have been proud of us. Not only did we work on saving the birds of Stoneybrook but we saved a few bugs, too.

Kristy baby-sits for the Kormans often because they're neighbors. The Kormans live across the street and one house down from the Brewer mansion. Their house is really huge, too, but much fancier than Kristy's. It used to belong to the Delaneys, who spent tons of money on really outrageous things. For instance, they put this big fish fountain in their front hallway. They also installed an immense swimming pool and a clay tennis court in their backyard. They put gold faucets in the bathrooms and fancy furniture in all of the rooms. And there are a lot of rooms!

Anyway, the Kormans live there now and they are really nice. Mr. and Mrs. Korman have three great kids — Bill (who's nine), Melody (who's seven), and little Skylar (who is one-and-a-half). Not too long after they moved to Stoneybrook, Melody became good friends with Kristy's stepsister, Karen.

The kids are a lot of fun and have active imaginations. Usually that's good, but now and then it makes for some unusual problems. Right after they moved in, Bill and Melody decided that a monster lived in their bathroom. (Actually, Mary Anne had sort of helped them come up with the idea the first time she baby-sat for the Kormans.)

In the beginning the kids had had fun inventing goofy monsters, like the hot dog monster, the tickle monster, and the tiptoe monster. But the toilet monster created all sorts of problems. The kids were afraid to go near the bathroom. They'd hide in their rooms listening to the gurgling sounds coming from the toilet and be too scared to go to sleep. Luckily for everyone, the Kormans finally called a plumber and got the pipes fixed. That took care of the toilet monster forever.

On this Tuesday afternoon, the Korman kids weren't thinking about monsters of any kind. They were too busy cutting up milk cartons and painting them.

"Hi!" Mrs. Korman greeted Kristy at the front door. "We're in the kitchen making a huge mess. Come on in."

"It's not a mess," Bill said as Kristy entered the kitchen. He was kneeling on newspapers that had been spread across the floor. "We're building bird houses. These are very important."

"That's right," Melody said as she squeezed a bottle of white glue onto the edge of a milk carton. "We're saving the animals of the planet."

"Let me guess," Kristy said, flipping the brim of her baseball cap up as she knelt beside the kids. "This is for Dawn and Stacey's class. Am I right?"

"Right!" Bill and Melody said at the same time.

Another voice joined in the chorus, shouting, "Wight!" That was Skylar. She was sitting in her high chair, with a handful of Cheerios on the tray in front of her, eagerly watching her brother and sister.

"This class has been great for the kids," Mrs. Korman said as she gathered her purse and sweater and pulled out her car keys. "Melody and Bill have made a lot of new friends and they're learning some really valuable lessons."

Kristy nodded. "Dawn and Stacey's class has changed a lot of people's lives."

Mrs. Korman put one hand over her mouth and whispered, "Of course, at times it's been a little awkward. The children watch us like hawks. Last week I threw an aluminum can in the garbage and Bill spent three days lecturing me about it."

"I know what you mean," Kristy whispered back with a grin. "Karen and Andrew and David Michael have been acting the same way at our house. They're driving everyone crazy. But I guess it's good for us."

"I guess so."

Mrs. Korman gave Kristy the number where she could be reached, and left instructions for dinner. "There are applesauce and cottage cheese in the fridge, and you can make the kids — "

"Hot dogs." Bill finished her sentence without even looking up.

"Well . . . yes," Mrs. Korman blinked her eyes in surprise. "How did you know?"

"We *always* eat hot dogs when baby-sitters are here," Melody groaned.

"But I thought you liked hot dogs."

"We do," Bill said. "But not all the time."

Mrs. Korman pursed her lips. "Well, there's a frozen pizza in the refrigerator. Would you rather eat that?"

"Yea!" Bill raised his paintbrush and cheered.

Their mother shrugged. "Then pizza it is. I'll see you later."

After Mrs. Korman left, Kristy removed the pizza from the freezer, checked the cooking instructions, and set the oven to 350° to preheat it. "It looks like we only have twenty minutes before we'll need to clean up and eat dinner," she warned Bill and Melody.

"That's okay," Melody said, sprinkling glitter on the glue design she'd made on the outside of her bird house. "My bird house should be finished by then."

"I want to cut out one more bird house before we stop," Bill said. "Kristy, would you help me?"

"Sure." Kristy knelt beside him. "Just tell me what to do."

"Okay." Bill handed her a milk carton. "What you see before you looks like an ordinary milk carton, but wait and see what can happen with a pair of scissors, a roll of tape, a piece of wire, and two nails."

Kristy turned to Melody. "It sounds like he's rehearsed this speech."

"He has," Melody said, rolling her eyes. "Over and over again. He'll be giving it at his booth at the Green Fair."

Bill held the carton upside down. "First we make sure the carton is clean — that there's no trace of milk left inside. Then we tear open the top. Then we take the scissors and cut out a hole about the size of a doorknob." He lowered his voice confidentially. "That'll be the birdies' front door."

"Tweet! Tweet!" Skylar cried.

"Now we turn the carton around," Bill continued, "punch two holes in the back, and loop this wire through them."

Kristy was impressed with how skillful Bill was.

"And then we seal up the carton."

"Wait!" Melody cried. "You forgot the most important part — the dried grass."

"Yikes!" Bill grabbed a handful of the grass clippings piled on one corner of the newspa-

116

pers and dropped them inside the carton. Then he said, in a much louder voice, "*Now* we tape the top of the carton closed."

"You can decorate the outside any way you want," Melody said, pointing to her own handiwork.

"And then you pound two nails into a tree," Bill added, "and tie the wires around the nails."

"Then what?" Kristy asked.

Bill smiled. "Then you sit back and wait for a bird family to move in."

"Make sure you hang the carton high enough on the tree that cats can't get at it," Melody warned.

"Tat!" Skylar squawked. "No tats. No tats."

Kristy remembered then that Skylar is afraid of cats. Just hearing one mentioned could set her off for fifteen minutes. Kristy hurried to the high chair and smoothed Skylar's hair. "Don't worry. There aren't any cats here."

"No tats!" Skylar whimpered.

"Right," Kristy said. "And just to be on the safe side . . ." Kristy crossed to the Kormans' back door, opened it, and yelled, "Go away, cats. We don't want you here."

Skylar stared wide-eyed at Kristy, who explained, "I've just told all the cats to leave. No cats will come here again."

As she spoke, Kristy crossed her fingers behind her back, silently hoping that Boo-Boo, Watson's seventeen-pound tomcat, would never make his way into the Kormans' yard.

"My bird house is finished," Bill announced, holding the carton in the air. He'd drawn blue stars all over it with a colored marker. "That makes six."

"Great!" said Kristy. "Now I'll put the pizza in the oven while you kids clean up."

"We can't clean everything up," Melody said. "Because we have to make the tree feeders for *my* booth — the plant sale booth."

"Tree feeders?" Kristy repeated. "Are they made out of milk cartons?"

"No!" Melody laughed. "They're made out of trees and food."

"Twees and foo!" Skylar repeated.

This time it was Melody's turn to demonstrate. "You see, during the winter, the birds get really hungry. And they don't have any bird grocery stores that they can go to for food. So by using our garbage we can feed them."

"Garbage? You mean, like tin cans and stuff?"

"No." Melody shook her head. "Garbage you can eat. Like orange peels — birds love that. And bread crusts."

"You can also make bird snacks by filling a pinecone with peanut butter," Bill pointed out.

"Pealut butter!" Skylar yelled.

"Skylar loves peanut butter," Melody whispered. "Now that we mentioned it, I think you'll have to give her some. Mom puts it on a graham cracker."

While Kristy went to the cupboard, Melody continued to explain her tree feeder. "You can tie strings around the pinecones, or bread crusts, or orange peels, and hang them from a tree."

"Outside your window is a good place," Bill said, pointing to an evergreen that was framed by their big kitchen window. "That way you can watch the birds eat. You can also tie strings around peanuts."

"Sounds like decorating a Christmas tree," Kristy observed.

"Only this tree is alive," Bill said. "We're saving the birds and the trees at the same time."

"Did you learn this in Dawn and Stacey's class?" Kristy asked.

The kids nodded.

"We've been learning how to protect the animals," Melody added. "Even the yuckiest worm or spider."

"How can you protect the spiders?" Kristy asked as the timer went off on the kitchen stove.

"Well, the next time you see a spider crawling up the wall or across your kitchen counter, don't squish it," Bill said. "You're supposed to take them outside and let them go."

"Really?" Kristy said.

"Spiders are great," Melody added. "Without them we'd be overrun with bugs."

"Did you know that the bugs spiders eat in one year weigh as much as all of the people on the earth?" Bill said.

Kristy wrinkled her nose in disgust. "That's a lot of bugs."

Kristy opened the oven and inspected the pizza. After the talk about bugs taking over the planet and squishing spiders, she had lost her appetite. But she didn't want the kids to know that. Instead she said, "This looks delicious. Okay. Sit down at the table. I'll serve the pizza, and you can tell me more about saving the earth's birds."

She put heavy emphasis on the word bird, hoping to steer the kids away from the subject of squashing bugs and spiders. It worked. Kristy was finally able to choke down a piece of pizza (even though the black olives on the pizza looked a whole lot like little beetles).

After dinner Kristy moved Skylar to her playpen and the kids spent another two hours making bird houses. Kristy had brought her Kid-Kit with her and it contained a set of water colors and a box of crayons. Bill built the bird houses and she and Melody decorated them. By the time Mrs. Korman came home, they had completed fifteen.

"Mom! Look what we did!" Bill shouted. "My booth is going to be the best one at the fair."

Melody hopped in a circle around her mother shouting, "Can Kristy come back tomorrow? I'm making some more signs for *my* booth. And I'm going to finish making the evergreen trees into tree feeders. Can Kristy come back and help? Can she?"

Mrs. Korman gave Melody a hug. "Of course she can, but I'll bet Kristy is pretty busy."

Kristy had enjoyed working on the bird houses. Since she had the next afternoon free, she said, "I'd love to help you, Melody. But I'll do it on one condition."

"What's that?" Melody asked.

"If you promise that we don't talk about squashing bugs while we're working."

Melody solemnly put one hand over her heart. "I promise. No bugs."

"And no tats," Skylar called from her playpen.

Kristy picked her up and gave her a squeeze. "Then it's a deal. I'll see you all tomorrow."

CHAPTER 13

Wednesday. Three days before the Green Fair. It seemed as though we still had a million things to do before Saturday. I rode to the BSC meeting with posters and fliers and name tags filling the basket on my bicycle. Mary Anne had baby-sat for the Marshalls that afternoon and she met me on Claud's front porch.

"Need some help?" she asked.

"Yes!" I exclaimed. "The editor at the newspaper needs to be called, the booths still aren't ready, I'm not sure if all the kids have finished their projects, and I'm going to need someone to videotape the event."

Mary Anne's mouth fell open. "I meant, do you need help carrying those posters upstairs?"

"Oh. Sure." I would have been embarrassed if it had been anybody but Mary Anne. Instead

I chuckled. "I thought you were talking about the Green Fair."

Mary Anne helped me carry my posters and fliers up to Claud's room and then I passed them out as quickly as I could.

"Nice artwork!" Kristy said as she read the poster I handed her.

I gestured grandly to Claudia. "We can thank Ms. Kishi for that."

Just then the digital clock changed from 5:29 to 5:30. Kristy leaned back in the director's chair and announced, "All right. The BSC is officially called to order. Is there any club business we need to discuss?"

"Yes," I said. "I've just given you each five posters, twenty fliers, and a name tag."

Jessi held up her poster. "What are we supposed to do with these?"

"I want you to put them up around town. There are seven of us, so we can put up thirty-five posters. And Mary Anne, if Logan can take five, that'll be forty."

"You want us to put them in grocery store windows, and places like that?" Claud asked.

"Right. Now I've made a list of places for each of you to take the posters. You have to have them up by tomorrow afternoon or — "

"Hold it!" Kristy interrupted. "I can't. I'm busy tomorrow."

"What?" I dropped my arms to my sides. "Kristy, I was counting on you. You've got to put your posters in the library and the art museum."

"How could you count on me when you never talked to me about this before?" Kristy protested.

"Oh, never mind. I'll just do yours myself." I took back her posters and tossed them on the bed.

Kristy shrugged apologetically. "Sorry. But I didn't know anything about it."

Stacey leaned forward from her seat on the bed. "Don't worry, Kristy," she began. "We'll — "

"Talk about it later?" I finished in an irritated voice. "We don't have much time. A client could call at any moment."

"Sorry." Stacey pressed her lips together and leaned back against the wall.

"Now I want you all to be sure to wear these name tags on Saturday," I said, pointing to the labels I'd carefully lettered in colored markers.

"Why do we need to wear name tags?" Mal asked.

I sighed. "Because," I said, overemphasizing each word, "you're all going to be helping at the fair, aren't you?"

Mal and Jessi looked at each other with raised eyebrows. Then Jessi said, "Nobody told me about it."

"What?" This time I turned to Stacey and practically shouted, "I thought you were going to give them their assignments."

"Correction," Stacey said through clenched teeth. "I was going to *ask* them if they would like to help us on Saturday."

I folded my arms across my chest. "Well, of course they want to help us. They're our friends, aren't they?"

"Yes, and friends *ask* friends first," Stacey shot back. "They don't order them around."

I turned to the rest of the club members. "I'm not ordering you around, am I?"

For a few moments everyone was silent. No one looked me in the eye. Finally Kristy said, "Yes. You've been firing orders at us since the meeting started."

"That's not true," I huffed.

"Oh, yes it is," Stacey declared, raising up on her knees. "And furthermore, you've been barking orders at me ever since we started this whole stupid ecology project."

"Oh, I get it," I said sarcastically. "You think ecology is stupid? Well, no wonder you haven't been doing your share of the work."

"How could I?" Stacey retorted. "You've

been doing it for me. You think you're the only one who knows anything about pollution."

"Well, I have done a lot of research."

"So have I," Stacey pointed out. "We take the same science class, remember? We've read the same books. Who suggested we use the book *50 Simple Things Kids Can Do to Save the Earth*? Me. I read it first."

"Yes, but — "

"To hear you talk, you'd think I wasn't even involved in this project. Or worse, that I was just one of the kids in our class. You've been bossing me around from the beginning and I'm tired of it." Stacey folded her arms firmly across her chest. "And I'm not going to let you boss our friends around."

"I don't boss people around," I protested.

"Yes, you do," Claud said from across the room. "Ever since you started this ecology project you've been telling me what to eat."

"And telling me what kind of paper to buy, and how much to use," Mary Anne added.

Kristy nodded. "And you acted as if I committed murder when I accidentally threw away a soda can."

"But that's only because it's so important to recycle if we want the planet to survive." I looked from Kristy to Claudia to Mary Anne.

"Someone has to tell people what they're doing wrong."

"We know that," Claudia said. "But you've gone from being a teacher to being a policewoman. You expect everybody to be perfect, and you make us feel like criminals."

"And it's really not very pleasant," Mary Anne added.

"In fact," Kristy said, "it's obnoxious."

There was that word again. The same one I had heard Cokie Mason use the day of the elections. I couldn't believe my ears. My very own friends were turning against me.

A lump began to form in the back of my throat but I was determined not to cry. Luckily, the phone rang and I didn't have to say anything right away.

Mal answered it. Mrs. Newton needed a sitter for Jamie and Lucy on Saturday morning. Mary Anne checked the record book. "Stacey and Dawn are busy with the Green Fair," she said, "and Mal and Jessi are sitting for the Pikes, so that leaves Kristy, Claud, or me."

"I'll take it," Claud volunteered. With a sideways glance at me she added, "But don't worry, Dawn. I'll be sure and bring the kids to the Green Fair."

I tried to smile but I was still reeling from what everyone had said to me. I knew I had been pretty insistent about recycling but I never dreamed anyone would think I was bossy and obnoxious. If my best friends felt that way about me, no wonder the kids at school had voted for Mrs. Gonzalez.

After Mal called Mrs. Newton back to tell her that Claud would be sitting for her, the room was silent once more. I knew everyone was waiting to hear my response to what they had said.

I couldn't look at anybody. I just stared down at my hands and murmured, "I had no idea you guys were so upset with me."

Mary Anne touched my arm gently. "Look, Dawn, we know you meant well but you can't force people to think like you do."

"Mary Anne's right," Claudia added. "Nobody likes being told what to do."

I thought about the things I'd said to people, at home, at school, and at the BSC meetings, over the past few weeks. I realized I had been awfully pushy.

"I — I'm sorry, you guys," I stammered. "I never — "

"Wait a minute, Dawn," Mary Anne interrupted. "We're not finished."

I bit my lip and waited for her to tell me what else I'd been doing wrong."

"We want you to know," Mary Anne continued, "that even though Mrs. Gonzalez has done a great job of pulling together the recycling project, we think you should be in charge."

"But only if you change your attitude," Kristy added. "You know, approach it like a sane person."

"Yeah, not like the eco-maniac you've been," Claud joked.

Everyone giggled at Claud's words. Even me. "I guess I have been a little overbearing."

"A little!" Stacey repeated. "You've been like a bulldozer, mowing down everyone who's ever used a plastic bag or had a drink from a Styrofoam cup. Which, I might add, is practically everybody."

I had to admit it, Stacey was right. I had spent the last few weeks feeling angry with everyone because they wouldn't shape up immediately. And I had been unfair to Stacey, taking over our classes as if she weren't even involved, and then ordering her around.

"Stacey, I'm really sorry I've been so awful to you."

"That's all right," Stacey said. "I should have told you how I was feeling a long time ago."

"Look," I said, "I know there are only three days left before the Green Fair, but I promise to make those three days fun and not be a bossy jerk. Okay?"

Stacey grinned. "Sounds good to me."

"Then are we still friends?"

I stuck out my hand and Stacey shook it.

"We're still friends."

"Great." I flopped on the bed next to her. "Then we should start work on our report for Mrs. Gonzalez's class. I've made an outline — "

"*Dawn!*" everyone shouted.

I nearly fell off the bed. "What?" I asked.

"You're doing it again!" Claudia said.

"Oops." I covered my mouth with my hand. "I guess I should have said, when would you like to start work on our report?"

Stacey grinned at me. "As soon as we can. I've written an outline, too. Let's put them together and see what we come up with."

"Perfect!" I declared. I threw my arms around Stacey. Behind me I could hear Jessi whisper to Mal, "Don't you just love happy endings?"

CHAPTER 14

"Save a tree!"

"Write the President!"

"Kids care!"

It was Saturday, the day of our Green Fair, and you could hear the kids calling from their booths all the way down the street.

I'd slept at Stacey's the night before, so we could get up bright and early to make sure the booths were ready. We'd set the alarm for six o'clock but we were wide awake before that.

The fair was scheduled to begin at ten. At five to, Stacey clutched my arm in a panic. "What if nobody comes?"

That was something I hadn't even considered. For one brief second my pulse raced with fear. Then I said, "We've got thirteen kids involved and they all have parents who are coming. Then there's the BSC — they promised to be here."

"What if too *many* people come?" Stacey gasped. "My yard isn't that big!"

I draped my arm over her shoulder. "Stop worrying. Things are probably going to go wrong, but if we stay calm we can handle them."

Moments later I had to eat my words as a gust of wind lifted the Kids Care button booth four feet in the air and dropped it in a heap around Karen, Andrew, and Suzi.

"Help!" Karen cried. "We've been smushed." The booth, which was really just a couple of cardboard refrigerator boxes stapled together, had ripped apart. Large pieces of cardboard lay on the ground.

"Our booth is ruined," Suzi Barrett wailed.

"No, it's not," Stacey said.

"Yes, it is." Andrew grumbled as he dragged the button making machine out from under the cardboard. "No one will want to come to it."

"Now what kind of an attitude is that?" I said as I tried to prop the booth back up. "All we need is a little tape and a staple gun, and this booth will be as good as new."

Fortunately for us, Mallory and Jessi entered the yard just as the accident happened. Mal overheard me and shouted, "One staple gun and a roll of tape, coming right up." She sent Byron back to their house for the supplies, then brought the rest of her brothers and sisters over to join us.

"Wow!" Mal cried to Karen, Suzi, and Andrew. "I saw that wind lift your booth off the ground and spin it around. It looked like *The Wizard of Oz*, when Dorothy's house flies through the air."

"*The Wizard of Oz*?" Suzi's blue eyes widened. "Really?"

Jessi nodded. "Absolutely. It looked like magic."

"Magic!" the kids repeated. Then they turned to look back at the battered booth.

"It did feel sort of magical," Karen whispered to the others. "One second the air was still and the next a strange gust of wind lifted us up to the clouds."

"Yeah," Andrew answered in a hushed voice. "We were flying."

"Flying?" Adam Pike scoffed. But before he could say another word, Mal cupped her hand over his mouth.

"Our booth must be the most special one at the fair," Suzi Barrett concluded.

By this time Byron was back with the supplies and the kids could hardly wait to repair their "magical" booth.

I mouthed a grateful thanks to Mal, who shrugged and said, "It was nothing."

While Stacey helped to fix the button booth,

I glanced around to make sure none of the other booths had blown over. Stacey's backyard was already starting to fill with people. I noticed Claudia Kishi standing with Jamie and Lucy Newton in front of Linny and David Michael's demonstration booth. Linny was using grand gestures as he talked, when suddenly he stopped speaking and shouted, "Oh, no!"

I hurried across the lawn to see what had gone wrong. By the time I arrived the two boys were involved in a heated argument.

"I thought you were going to bring it!" David Michael said.

"No, *you* were supposed to bring it," Linny replied.

"Hey, you guys, cool down," Claudia said. "There's no need to fight."

"What's going on?" I asked.

David Michael poked his finger at Linny. "*He* was supposed to bring the celery for our It Came from Underground demonstration."

"I was not," Linny said, shaking his head violently. "*He* was supposed to bring it."

"Why do you need celery?" Jamie Newton asked the boys.

"Because we want to show that polluted water also wrecks the trees," David Michael explained.

"You're going to show that with celery?" Jamie looked dubious.

"Sure," David Michael replied. "You see, we get this glass of water and we put red food coloring in it."

"That's the pollution," Linny explained.

"Then we stick the celery, which is supposed to represent a tree, in the water."

"And then what?" Jamie asked.

"Then comes the really cool part," Linny said. "You can actually watch the red water climb up the stalk of celery."

"That sounds neat," Jamie said to Claud. "I want to see."

David Michael scowled. "Well, you can't because *he* forgot the celery."

I held up my hands. "Now let's not start that again. If all you need is a stalk of celery, Stacey's probably got a ton of it in her refrigerator. Linny, why don't you run inside and ask Mrs. McGill to give you a stalk? And while you do that, David Michael can demonstrate the buried treasure experiment."

The boys looked at each other for a second, and then smiled. "Okay."

"How's it going?" Claud whispered as David Michael began his speech.

"We're off to a shaky start," I replied. "But I think everything's going to be just fine."

"You're getting a good crowd," Claud pointed out. "Look, Mary Anne brought the twins."

Marilyn and Carolyn, who are identical eight-year-olds, stood side by side in front of Charlotte and Becca's shopping bag booth. Each was busily decorating her own canvas bag. Mary Anne stood a little distance away, talking to Mrs. Addison, who had brought her daughter Corrie to the fair.

After checking to make sure Nicky and Vanessa's letter writing campaign was under control, I joined Mary Anne. She greeted me with a hug. "This fair is fantastic. You and Stacey are geniuses."

"Mary Anne's right," Mrs. Addison added. "I'm overwhelmed at all the good information that's being handed out here."

Before I could reply, Marilyn and Carolyn joined us. "Look, Mary Anne," Marilyn called, holding up her bag. "I decorated this myself."

On her bag the words, *I Saved a Tree* were written in pink and blue paint across one side. Marilyn had glued little sequins to the word "tree." On the other side of the bag she had painted her name.

Carolyn rushed to Mary Anne, clutching her own bag, which was painted green and yellow. "Did you know that paper bags are made from trees? And one fifteen-year-old tree makes seven hundred bags?"

"Wow!" Mary Anne said. "That's a lot of bags."

Marilyn shook her head. "But it's really not. Because a grocery store can go through that many bags in one hour."

Carolyn held up her bag. "That's why it's important to use canvas bags."

Mrs. Addison, who was admiring the bags, asked, "Where did you learn all that?"

Marilyn and Carolyn turned and pointed. "At the shopping bag booth. Melody and Hannie told us."

"That's amazing," Mrs. Addison exclaimed.

I squeezed Mary Anne's hand. "Isn't it? I'm so proud of the kids. They're all doing so well."

"You should be proud," a familiar voice said. "I've been watching a demonstration on how to make tree feeders, and I can't wait to go home and make one myself."

I spun around and found myself face to face with my science teacher. "Mrs. Gonzalez!" I gasped. "I'm glad you could come."

Mrs. Gonzalez smiled. "I wouldn't have missed this for the world."

"Dawn!" Bill Korman shouted from his booth. "Dawn, come quick!"

"Oops," I said. "It looks like trouble's brewing at the wild animal booth. Excuse me."

"If you don't mind," Mrs. Gonzalez said, "I'll go with you."

My heart sank. I expected to find something terribly wrong at the boys' booth.

But when Mrs. Gonzalez and I got there, Bill and Buddy were grinning from ear to ear.

"What's the matter, Bill?" I asked.

"We just sold ten bird houses," Buddy cried with glee.

"What's wrong with that?" I asked.

"Nothing," Bill replied, looked slightly confused. "We thought it was great news."

"Yeah," Buddy added. "Do you know how much money we've made?"

Stacey, the math whiz, came up beside me and answered, "Twenty dollars. Great work, guys!"

Bill pointed to the line of kids forming in front of their booth. "At this rate, we'll make a hundred dollars by the time the fair's over."

"That's a lot of money," Mrs. Gonzalez said, obviously impressed. "What do you plan to do with it?"

"We're going to give it to an environmental organization," Stacey explained. "But we haven't chosen one yet."

Suddenly I got an idea. "I know which one I'd like to give it to," I said to Stacey. "But I want to talk it over with you first."

Stacey smiled at me. "Whichever one you choose is fine with me."

"Are you sure?" I asked, "I mean, I don't want to be pushy or anything."

Stacey giggled. "You're not being pushy. Who do you want to give it to?"

I dug my toe in the ground as I talked. "I've done a lot of thinking. You know, the world has a lot of wonderful ecological organizations like The Environmental Defense Fund and Greenpeace, but one of the lessons I've learned over the past six weeks is that helping the planet begins at home. So . . ." I took a deep breath. "I move we donate the proceeds from our Green Fair to Stoneybrook Middle School's recycling project."

Stacey smiled. "That's a great idea. I second the motion."

"All in favor?" I asked. Then we giggled as we said, "Aye."

Stacey turned to Mrs. Gonzalez. "Okay, it's official. The money from our Green Fair will go to the recycling project."

"That," said Mrs. Gonzalez, "is the best idea I've heard today."

CHAPTER 15

"Thirty pages!" Stacey gasped as the copier machine at the print shop churned out our report for Mrs. Gonzalez. "Can you believe it? This is practically a book!"

As the pages came out of the copier, I separated them into two neat piles. "It would probably have been longer if we had included the extra research we did on rain forests."

We were making two copies of our report because Stacey and I were in different classes. We had also decided to include a one page essay on what we had learned individually from participating in the project.

"I hope Mrs. Gonzalez is impressed by this," Stacey said as she handed me a green cover. I'd chosen the color to represent the earth and the green trees. Stacey's cover was blue, which she said represented the oceans and clean drinking water.

"She better be impressed," I replied. "Just

typing this took a whole week."

After Stacey and I had attached the covers to our reports, we went over to her house to celebrate. Her mom had bought us a bottle of sparkling cider just for the occasion.

Stacey popped the cork and poured the cider into two of her mother's expensive Waterford crystal glasses. We took our drinks into the living room and then I proposed a toast.

"Here's to you," I declared, holding up my glass. "For putting up with bossy old me for six weeks."

Stacey raised her glass. "And here's to you, for thinking up the best project in the whole school."

We clinked glasses and Stacey added, "I hope we get an A."

"Of course we'll get an A," I said, after taking a sip of my cider. "We deserve it."

But when I turned in my copy of the report the next morning, I didn't feel nearly as confident as I had the night before.

"What if she says my report's too long?" I whispered to Amelia after I placed my report on Mrs. Gonzalez's desk.

"Who knows? It might be too short," Elizabeth replied. "Did you see Pete Black's report? It's so huge, it must weigh five pounds."

"Maybe my essay is all wrong," I mumbled to myself as I hurried back to my desk.

I spent the next seven days worrying about that report. I know that sounds silly, especially after all the work Stacey and I had done. It was my essay that worried me the most. Stacey told me she had written her essay on how she planned to stay involved in the ecology movement in the future. I didn't even mention the word ecology or pollution in mine.

The following Monday, Mrs. Gonzalez appeared in science class with a stack of papers in her arms. Everyone knew what they were — the reports. But she didn't hand them out right away. She made us suffer first. Then during the last ten minutes of class she passed them back to us.

My hands were shaking so much I could barely open mine. All around me I heard excited cries and disappointed sighs, as people saw their grades. But still I couldn't bring myself to open the cover. I finally got up the nerve when the bell rang. I squeezed my eyes shut and, quick, flipped open the cover. I couldn't believe what I saw.

Written in bright red ink was the letter A. Next to it was this note from Mrs. Gonzalez:

"Your project was superb and this report is excellent. Carefully thought out, well-executed, and a delight to read. Especially the essay. Please see me after class — I'd like to talk to you."

When I looked up from my paper, I discovered I was the only student left in the classroom. Mrs. Gonzalez was standing in front of her desk.

"Well?" she asked. "Are you happy?"

"Am I happy?" I repeated. "I could jump for joy!"

"Go ahead," she chuckled. "No one's watching, and I won't tell."

(In case you're wondering I did *not* jump, but I did do a lot of squealing with happiness — later on, when I told the rest of the BSC at lunch. And that was because of what Mrs. Gonzalez said to me next.)

"Dawn," she began, taking a seat, "I know you were disappointed when the school chose me to head the recycling center."

I started to protest, but Mrs. Gonzalez said, "It's okay. I would have been upset, too. After all, it was your idea."

I looked down at my hands. "Well, maybe I was a *little* disappointed."

"I have a proposal that I'd like to put in front of the student body. Mr. Kingbridge thinks it's a good idea. All we need is for the students to say yes."

"What is it?"

"I'd like you to co-chair the recycling program with me."

I couldn't believe my ears. "Really?"

Mrs. Gonzalez nodded. "That means we split everything — good and bad jobs alike — fifty-fifty. It would also mean that you'd have to give up a lot of Saturdays so you could supervise the project."

"That's fine with me," I said. "When do we start?"

"As soon as the students vote on it."

"Oh." My shoulders drooped. "I don't think they'll want me, not after the way I've behaved."

"I'll admit you were a little overexuberant at first," Mrs. Gonzalez said carefully.

"My friends said I was obnoxious," I blurted out.

That made her laugh. "Well, maybe just a little bit," she admitted. "But it was for a good cause. Besides, you've changed."

"Do you really think so?" I said hopefully.

"I can see it and so can the students. So what do you say?"

"Well . . . sure," I replied. "And I'll keep my fingers crossed that they'll want me."

"Oh, they'll want you," Mrs. Gonzalez assured me, patting my hand. "I haven't a single doubt about it."

Well, after getting an A on my report, plus the offer to co-chair the project, I was flying. At lunchtime I raced all the way to the cafeteria. Stacey was waiting to greet me.

"We did it!" she cried.

I wrapped my arms around her and squealed, "We got an A!"

"Of course, you got an A," Claud said matter-of-factly from behind us.

"Absolutely!" Kristy set her hamburger and fries on the table and slid into a chair. "Your project was pure genius!"

I waited until Mary Anne and Logan joined the table to make my big announcement. "Mrs. Gonzalez asked me to co-chair the recycling project."

"Yes!" Mary Anne squealed.

"All right!" Kristy said, giving me a high five.

"Don't get too excited," I warned them. "The school has to vote on it first, and you know what happened last time."

"That's all in the past," Claud replied. "This time I'm sure they'll elect you."

"I hope you're right," I said. "Mrs. Gonzalez said that after reading my essay, she'd decided I'd changed for the better."

"What *did* you say in your essay?" Stacey asked, raising a piece of celery to her mouth. "I never read yours."

"Well, I titled it *Saving the Planet — You Can't Do It Alone*. Then I described how working on the project turned me into a bossy jerk. I said how I got so self-righteous and obnoxious that no one, not even my friends in the Baby-sitters Club, wanted to help me." I smiled at Stacey and added, "I also mentioned what a saint you were for putting up with me."

"Oh, Dawn! "That's not true."

"Your paper sounds more like True Confessions than an essay," Claudia said. "Did Mrs. Gonzalez like it?"

"She loved it. She especially liked the ending where I wrote — " I pulled my report out of my book bag and, flipping to the last page, read out loud, "I've discovered that in order to make big changes in the world we have to begin at home — within ourselves. Now that I've begun to clean up my own act, I think I'll be better equipped to help others clean up the world."

"Gee, Dawn," Mary Anne said after a few moments of silence, "that was really great."

"It's the truth," I said with a shrug. "I mean, look at the BSC. It's a success because we work together." I looked around the table and realized how proud I was to have such good friends. "And when you work together, you can do almost anything. Even save a planet."

Dear Reader,

In *Dawn Saves the Planet*, Dawn's friends get mad at her because they think Dawn is going overboard with her efforts to make everyone environmentally aware. But the truth is, it doesn't take much to make a difference. Here are some quick and easy things you can do to help save the planet:

- Turn off lights, the radio, or the television when you leave a room.
- Reuse items as often as you can, and then recycle them, if possible.
- Don't leave water running in the sink.
- If your community has a recycling program, save and recycle newspapers, cans, and bottles. (I recycle dozens of cat food cans a week.)
- Buy refillable products whenever possible, such as cleaners and lotions.
- Use reusable products whenever possible— cloth instead of paper napkins and towels, china instead of paper plates, etc.

These things may seem simple, and they are. Little things really do make a difference.

Happy reading,

Ann M Martin

L. GODWIN

Ann M. Martin

About the Author

ANN MATTHEWS MARTIN was born on August 12, 1955. She grew up in Princeton, NJ, with her parents and her younger sister, Jane.

Although Ann used to be a teacher and then an editor of children's books, she's now a full-time writer. She gets the ideas for her books from many different places. Some are based on personal experiences. Others are based on childhood memories and feelings. Many are written about contemporary problems or events.

All of Ann's characters, even the members of the Baby-sitters Club, are made up. (So is Stoneybrook.) But many of her characters are based on real people. Sometimes Ann names her characters after people she knows, other times she chooses names she likes.

In addition to the Baby-sitters Club books, Ann Martin has written many other books for children. Her favorite is *Ten Kids, No Pets* because she loves big families and she loves animals. Her favorite Baby-sitters Club book is *Kristy's Big Day*. (By the way, Kristy is her favorite baby-sitter!)

Ann M. Martin now lives in New York with her cats, Gussie and Woody. Her hobbies are reading, sewing, and needlework — especially making clothes for children.

Notebook Pages

This Baby-sitters Club book belongs to _____ .

I am _____ years old and in the _____

grade.

The name of my school is _____ .

I got this BSC book from _____ .

I started reading it on _____ and

finished reading it on _____ .

The place where I read most of this book is _____ .

My favorite part was when _____ .

If I could change anything in the story, it might be the part when

_____ .

My favorite character in the Baby-sitters Club is _____ .

The BSC member I am most like is _____ .

because _____ .

If I could write a Baby-sitters Club book it would be about ___

_____ .

#57 Dawn Saves the Planet

Environmental issues are very important to Dawn and the other BSC members. To help save the planet, they recycle, respect wildlife, and collect litter. Some things I would like to do to help the environment are _____

_____

_____

_____

Stacey and Dawn organize a Green Fair as part of their Save the Planet class. If I had participated in the Green Fair, this is what I would have done: _____

_____

_____. Dawn takes a stand and helps to start a recycling center in her school. Some changes I would like to make in my school are _____

_____

_____. The friends who would help me are _____

_____.

DAWN'S

Back and forth
between my two families.

Baby days in California.
Me at 1½.

My very own secret
passage -- and ghost.

SCRAPBOOK

The Impossible Three and me!

Starring the BSC-- tryouts for _Peter Pan._

Illustrations by Angelo Tillery